N

I

[

JA

i

DEATH IN CAMERA

Michael Underwood
DEATH IN CAMERA

St. Martin's Press
New York

Library of Congress Cataloging in Publication Data

Underwood, Michael, 1916-
  Death in camera.

  I. Title.
PR6055.V3D4   1984   823'. 914   84-2112
ISBN 0-312-18612-6

First Published in Great Britain by Macmillan London Limited

First U.S. Edition

10 9 8 7 6 5 4 3 2 1

Chapter 1

The mayor droned on, viewing his captive audience with merciless relish. He enjoyed making speeches and could produce an unquenchable flow of platitudes for every occasion. Moreover, he regarded the opening of the new Runnymede Crown Court as one for pulling out all the stops in his oratorial repertoire. The more illustrious his audience, the greater his determination to impress; and what more illustrious than a gathering of judges and lawyers – or 'legal luminaries' as he persistently referred to them in his speech.

He was the final speaker and many of those who now filled the main court-room were casting less than surreptitious glances at their watches as his speech pursued its platitudinous course.

Speeches had been designed to last from twelve to twelve-thirty, after which there was a buffet lunch for invited guests. The three courts were due to begin their proper business of trying criminals at two o'clock.

Rosa Epton smothered a yawn and reflected that even a free lunch was going to be small recompense for listening to the mayor. She was involved in a big drugs case starting that afternoon before Mr Justice Ambrose and had accepted the invitation to the opening ceremony, as providing her with an opportunity to talk to the counsel she had briefed.

She glanced towards the judge, resplendent in his full-bottom wig and his ermine-trimmed scarlet robes and reflected what a forbidding figure he cut. Severe, humourless and autocratic: that was his reputation. She understood

5

that her case was originally in Judge Holtby's list, he being the senior of the two permanent judges assigned to the new court, but that Mr Justice Ambrose who was the visiting High Court judge, had peremptorily informed Leo Dodd, the hapless clerk of the court, that he intended trying it. When she sought the reason for the change she had been surprised by the tight-lippedness that met her innocent enquiry. Certainly Leo Dodd, normally of cheerful and carefree appearance, looked anything but happy at this moment as he sat on the dais next to Judge Welford, the court's other permanent judge. But Rosa supposed that could have been the effect of the mayor's speech.

'Hold on to your seats!' Rosa's neighbour murmured irreverently as the mayor launched into his peroration.

'It is particularly fitting that this magnificent court stands close to where Magna Carta was signed in 1215. Magna Carta, the ancient cornerstone of all our precious liberties,' he declaimed with an expansive gesture of his right hand. 'May all who practise in this court over seven centuries later be ever imbued by all that is finest in our legal heritage! May its judges dispense justice with mercy and may counsel uphold all that is best in the traditions of their proud profession!'

'And God bless all the defendants too!' murmured Rosa's neighbour.

The mayor sat down to a minimum of polite applause and there was a general movement towards the buffet, which was being served in a long room overlooking the Thames. Along one side french windows opened on to a balcony which overhung the river. On this particular March day a torrent of brown water swirled past, the result of several days of heavy rain which had been followed by a downfall of snow and an immediate thaw. But as if to make amends and show what a superb site had been chosen for the new court, the sun shone benignly and the cold north-easterly wind had given way to a balmy south-westerly breeze.

'What's happening now?' Rosa asked as she observed

6

various people being shepherded towards one of the large french windows.

'A photo call,' Jane Crenlow remarked drily. She was the Q.C. Rosa had briefed to defend her client in the drugs case.

'Oughtn't you to go and join all the legal luminaries?' Rosa said with a mischievous smile.

At that moment a voice called out, 'Miss Crenlow, you're wanted on the balcony.'

Jane Crenlow gave Rosa a look of mock despair and moved toward the french window.

As it was clear that neither food nor drink would be served until the photographic session was over, Rosa drifted across to watch. There seemed to be almost as many photographers as there were victims. Apart from professionals, wives and friends were active with expensive-looking bits of equipment.

In the centre of the line-up the mayor and Mr Justice Ambrose stood side by side, the one radiating social bonhomie, the other looking austere and disdainful. Leo Dodd, the clerk of the court, was next to the mayor, and their honours Judge Holtby and Judge Welford stood shoulder to shoulder on Mr Justice Ambrose's other side.

Was it Rosa's imagination or had they put space between themselves and his lordship? There was certainly a gap, but it was probably mere chance.

Bulbs flashed and cameras clicked and whirred as the photographers went into action. At that moment, too, as if to compete for attention, Concorde roared overhead two minutes out from Heathrow. Everyone looked up save Rosa, to whom Concorde was no longer a novelty, and who consequently was one of the few people present to observe the sudden startled expression on Mr Justice Ambrose's face. His right hand flew up to his neck at the very same moment as he toppled backwards over the stone balustrade and disappeared from view.

She ran to the edge of the balcony in time to see him being carried away downstream, his robes billowing out and giving

7

him the appearance of a large crimson bloodstain.

Almost immediately there was a confusion of shouts and somebody threw a lifebelt which swirled futilely away in a direction of its own. Meanwhile, before everyone's horrified gaze, Mr Justice Ambrose went bobbing and spinning on his way towards the weir.

'He can't swim,' Jane Crenlow said in a grim tone as she joined Rosa.

'He didn't seem to make any effort to save himself,' Rosa remarked.

Of one thing she was sure, Mr Justice Ambrose would not be taking his seat on the bench at two o'clock that day. Or any other day.

Chapter 2

'These prawn vol-au-vents are jolly good. Have one, Rosa!'

As he spoke, Paul Elson brushed enough crumbs from his waistcoat to feed a family of birds. He was a tubby, friendly man of around forty with four children who were small replicas of himself. More to the point he was the junior counsel Rosa had instructed in the defence of Bernard Blaker in the drugs case. She had briefed him many times before and had a high regard for his forensic astuteness. He and Jane Crenlow, his leader in the case, belonged to the same chambers and it was at her client's personal wish that Rosa had briefed Jane.

'I want you to get Miss Crenlow,' Blaker had said at his first meeting with Rosa. 'Any objections?'

Rosa had none, though Jane Crenlow was not somebody she had ever briefed before. But as Blaker was paying for his defence out of his own pocket he was certainly entitled to the counsel of his choice. It might have been a different matter if he were being defended at public expense.

Paul Elson waylaid a passing waitress and scooped up a handful of smoked salmon sandwiches.

'I seem to be the only person eating,' he remarked, gazing around the room. For the most part people were standing about in embarrassed groups picking equally nervously at food and conversation.

'Events have taken away most people's appetites,' Rosa observed drily.

9

'Not mine! Ambrose, J. was an old bastard on the bench and not much different off it. I'm not shedding any tears for the old so-and-so. Any barrister who did would be a hypocrite. Agreed, Jane?' he said turning to Jane Crenlow who had come up at that moment. He repeated for her benefit what he had said to Rosa.

'I wouldn't describe him as one of the more lustrous adornments on the bench,' Jane said cautiously.

Paul Elson grinned. 'There you are! Just what I said,' he exclaimed to Rosa. Turning back to Jane Crenlow he went on, 'Any news about what's happening to our case?'

'I gather there's to be an announcement at two o'clock. The rumour is that the courts won't sit today.'

'What about Mr Justice Ambrose?' Rosa asked. 'Have they managed to recover his body?'

Jane nodded. 'It was caught at the weir.'

At two o'clock Judge Holtby took his seat in a packed court. He was accompanied on the bench by Judge Welford who wore a grim expression. Holtby himself looked ashen and he had obvious difficulty keeping his voice under control.

'In view of this morning's tragedy, the court will adjourn immediately until tomorrow morning. I ask you all now to stand in silence for a minute as a mark of respect for Mr Justice Ambrose.'

As Paul Elson remarked afterwards, old Ambrose's Maker must have received quite a miscellany of pious and less than pious thoughts during this brief period. When the two judges had left the court, Leo Dodd came over to where counsel were standing.

'Blaker and others will start before Judge Holtby tomorrow morning,' he said with a tired smile. 'That is unless anything happens between now and then to prevent it.'

'You're not expecting a further depletion of the judiciary, are you?' Henry Keffingham asked in the mocking tone that came naturally to him.

10

'I certainly hope not,' Leo Dodd said in a tone of some alarm. 'I was just being ultra cautious.'

'I must say Tony Holtby looked as if he could do with a strong drink,' Keffingham went on thoughtfully.

'He's completely shattered by what's happened,' Dodd said.

'What about Stephen Welford, how's he taken it?' Keffingham asked with one quizzically raised eyebrow.

Dodd threw him a suspicious look. 'He's shocked like everyone else,' he said in a stony voice.

Henry Keffingham, Q.C. was briefed in the defence of Gail Bristow, the only female defendant in the drugs case. The remaining two defendants were Marcus Watt and Monty Yarfe, each of whom was separately represented. The prosecution was in the hands of Nicholas Barrow, Q.C. and Charles Rosten.

Briefly the case against the four defendants was that Bristow and Yarfe had been arrested at Heathrow airport on their arrival from Milan when approximately two kilos of cocaine, valued at £200,000, had been discovered in a vanity case Bristow had been about to retrieve when the officers swooped a fraction too soon, giving her the opportunity of disputing it was hers. She and Yarfe were travelling as Mr and Mrs Goodman, a wealthy Canadian couple on a honeymoon tour of Europe. Watt was the driver of the Daimler limousine which was waiting to pick them up. As for Bernard Blaker he had been an object of suspicion to the police for some time and was, to their certainty, at the centre of a drugs distribution racket whose profits amounted to over a million pounds a year. It was Watt who, in an effort to save his own skin, had given the police the information they needed to nail Blaker. The prosecution's hope was that Watt would plead guilty to a reduced charge and would thereafter turn Queen's Evidence against the others.

There had been much toing and froing behind the scenes with Watt under subtle, and sometimes less than subtle, pressure from both the police and shadowy figures on the opposite side. Even on the eve of the trial nobody was quite sure what was going to happen. The lawyers involved had, as was their wont, steered healthily clear of anything that could be construed as threats or inducements, conscious all the time, of course, of an ever powerful swell beneath the apparently calm water.

From the outset all four defendants had been on substantial bail, despite strenuous police opposition. They had surrendered to the court jailer that morning and were now in cells awaiting their release until the next day. In all the excitement and agitation, however, their presence in custody had been almost forgotten and Paul Elson now prepared to lead a deputation to see the clerk of the court and arrange a continuation of their bail.

Rosa, meanwhile, decided to go down to the cells and have a word with her client. She found him sitting in a cell which was as mint-fresh as the rest of the building. He was wearing the vicuna top-coat which she had come to regard as his trademark. It was unbuttoned to reveal a bluey-grey mohair suit and a cream silk shirt which had his initials monogrammed over his left nipple. He had once mentioned to Rosa in the course of casual conversation that he had his shirts made in Hong Kong and his suits in Italy. His shoes – a light burgundy – were, as always, beautifully polished and also, he had told her, came from Italy.

He got up as Rosa entered the cell.

'I gather there's been a hitch,' he said in his quiet, slightly sad voice.

'Yes, the judge who was due to try our case has been involved in an accident and been killed.'

'So who'll be trying it now?'

'Judge Holtby.'

He nodded thoughtfully. 'Is that a change for the better?'

'Certainly not for the worse,' Rosa remarked.

'I take it Miss Crenlow and Mr Elson have been here today?'

'Yes, both of them.'

Blaker gave a satisfied nod. 'Good.'

It was not often that Rosa found herself ill at ease with clients, but Bernie Blaker had that effect on her. She had tried to analyse her feelings and had come to the conclusion that it was because he was a genuinely evil man. If she accepted as true only part of all she had heard about him, he was wicked to the core. He had made a huge fortune out of the illicit drugs empire over which he reigned and was by all accounts totally ruthless and unscrupulous.

He was the sort of wealthy client (a flat in Mayfair and a large house near Weybridge, complete with indoor swimming pool and two gardeners' cottages) that firms like Snaith and Epton, which specialised in criminal work, often dreamt about, but Rosa had several times found herself wishing he had taken his business elsewhere.

At all their meetings and consultations with counsel he had never been less than polite. He always appeared to listen carefully to advice, but would then give his own view firmly and succinctly in his soft, sad voice. He was a handsome man with wavy iron grey hair and sad brown eyes which matched his voice. His complexion was sallow and though he was on the short side, he radiated power.

'Mr Elson's gone to attend to bail,' Rosa said. 'You'll be released shortly.'

He nodded again. Then with a sudden smile he said, 'I trust you have your fingers crossed for me, Miss Epton.'

'As your solicitor, I do much more than cross my fingers,' Rosa replied, uncertain how to respond to his remark.

'I appreciate all the work you've put into the case, Miss Epton,' he said. 'Some of my more chauvinistic friends think I must be soft in the head putting my fate into the hands of two women, but, so far, I've certainly no cause for regret. Miss Crenlow, of course, is only about to show off *her* paces, but I have as much confidence in her as I've always had in you.'

A number of replies flashed through Rosa's mind, but none of them seemed entirely right and so she said nothing.

13

Fortunately, what might have become an uncomfortable silence was broken by a prison officer opening the door and announcing that Blaker was free to leave but must be back at ten o'clock sharp the next morning.

A few minutes later, as Rosa manoeuvred her small Honda out of the car park, Bernie Blaker gave her a tiny wave from the back of his chauffeur-driven Mercedes as he also made his departure.

'I gather from the news that the opening of Runnymede Crown Court was accompanied by an unscripted drama,' Robin Snaith, her partner, said when Rosa returned to her office in West London.

'In front of my very eyes,' Rosa remarked with a small shiver.

'What actually happened?' he asked. When she had finished telling him he said, 'Have the police been on to you yet?'

'No.'

'They will be.'

'I imagine they're awaiting the results of the post mortem.'

'I wonder what caused his lordship to catapult backwards into the river? What's your theory?'

'I don't think I have one at the moment.' She paused and went on in a thoughtful tone, 'If he'd been shot, I'd have expected to have seen blood. Anyway, there wasn't any sound of a gun going off. I can only think he suddenly saw something that gave him such a shock that he lost his balance and toppled backwards.'

'It must have been some shock,' Robin observed. He shuffled some papers on his desk. 'We'll doubtless learn more soon enough.'

'Doubtless,' Rosa agreed as she walked slowly towards the door to go to her own room.

She just hoped that Mr Justice Ambrose's demise would not cast any deeper shadows over the trial that was about to start. It was going to be testing enough without any peripheral distractions.

Chapter 3

'I somehow don't think his lordship would be very happy to know I'm in charge of the enquiry into his death,' Detective Chief Superintendent Everson observed sardonically.

'I don't suppose he does know,' Detective Inspector Martin replied. 'He's probably too busy knocking on the pearly gates to look down.'

'Serve him right if his knuckles start bleeding. He tore my balls off in court once and I shan't forget it. Gave me the worst roasting I've ever had and now here I am charged with finding his murderer.'

'I suppose it is murder?' Martin said in a thoughtful voice.

'If you push somebody off a bridge and they drown, it's murder. And his lordship got something a darned sight more effective than a push. A pellet in his neck. And it's my bet that when it's examined it'll be found to contain poison. The same poison as killed that Bulgarian defector on Waterloo Bridge a few years ago.'

'Ricin.'

'Was that his name?'

'It's the name of the poison. It comes from the castor oil plant.'

'Find out all you can about it for me, David.'

'It was a bit of luck that Dr Berry noticed the mark on his neck.'

'He didn't. I did. It was no more than a small pimple, but when I drew his attention to it he dug out the pellet that was buried just beneath the skin. It's my guess it contained

15

enough poison to kill him off anyway.'

'Prompt first-aid and the right antidote might have saved his life.'

'Possibly. As it was, he filled his lungs with untreated Thames water which is more lethal than poison pellets. I wonder if his murderer knew he couldn't swim?'

'Any theories, sir, as to how the pellet was fired? The Bulgarian got his from an umbrella.'

'I fancy his lordship's came from a camera. Or what appeared to be a camera.'

'Ingenious.'

'So was the umbrella. In each case a specialist's weapon.'

D.I. Martin, who had been assigned to the case only an hour before and was having his first briefing, now asked the sixty-four thousand dollar question.

'Any idea who might have had a motive, sir?'

'The difficulty is finding somebody who didn't,' Everson remarked grimly. 'I understand his lordship recently threatened to report Henry Keffingham to the benchers of his Inn for unprofessional conduct in a case he was trying. And Keffingham is one of the defending counsel in a big drugs case that was scheduled to start before Ambrose yesterday afternoon. I've also learnt that his lordship had a row with Leo Dodd, the clerk of the court, when they met to discuss which cases should be tried by whom. He went so far as to suggest that Dodd wasn't up to his job. And then only just before you came into the room I was informed that Lady Ambrose left her husband three years ago and ran off with Judge Welford and is, in fact, now Mrs Welford.' He paused and fixed Inspector Martin with a sardonic gleam. 'How's that for starters?'

'I'm surprised Judge Welford wasn't required to resign. After all, judges are supposed to be like Caesar's wife, beyond reproach.'

'I don't know anything about Caesar's wife, but I do know that the legal establishment is capable of some pretty fancy footwork when it comes to covering up scandal within its own ranks.'

'So what's first on the agenda, sir?'

'A visit to Runnymede Crown Court. I want the names of everyone who took photographs on that balcony. I also want to have copies of all the photographs taken. They could reveal something of interest.'

Chapter 4

Judge Holtby was regarded as a fair though not particularly strong judge. He was inclined to be light on sentence, which didn't please the police, and he had a reputation for playing safe. That is to say, he would do everything he could to avoid being taken to the Court of Appeal.

He liked to tell people that he was aware of his limitations, which was an endearing trait in a profession not renowned for its corporate or individual modesty.

He was relaxed and easy-going without being lazy, though there were some who regarded him as a bit of a playboy. This label had become attached to him largely on account of his French wife. Denise was small and petite and had been an actress before her marriages – two marriages in fact. She was now in her early forties and the mother of four children, but still enjoyed the social whirl as much as she had in Paris when a girl. She had one son, Ian, by her first marriage, which had taken place when she was only seventeen.

Her first husband, who had been twenty years older than herself, had been a diplomat at the British Embassy at the time. Romantically enough they had met at an embassy ball. The marriage had lasted exactly six months and when Patrick Lester had been posted to Bogotá, she, by then six months pregnant, had remained in Paris.

She had met Tony Holtby when he came over as a member of a party of British barristers to play tennis against a team of French *avocats*. She had now been married to him for twenty years and they had three children, Charles aged nineteen,

18

Susan seventeen and Paul fourteen.

Though Tony Holtby had never taken formal steps to adopt his stepson, Ian had always been regarded as a full member of the family. Denise was known to be fiercely loyal to her husband and to be something of a tigress where her children were concerned.

'God, he looks ill,' Jane Crenlow murmured to Rosa when Judge Holtby took his seat on the bench that morning. 'Ambrose's death must have hit him really hard, not that they could ever have been friends. But I suppose it's understandable. It's a terrible thing to have happened and, as the senior resident judge, he obviously feels some sort of responsibility. A bit like a guest being murdered at your dinner table.'

Nobody arriving at Runnymede Crown Court that morning had been left in any doubt that Mr Justice Ambrose's death was no mere unfortunate accident. The whole building throbbed with rumour and speculation. People stood about in knots exchanging furtive whispers. Witnesses and jurors who foregathered in the spacious entrance hall could have been forgiven for thinking they had strayed into a temple in which strange mystical rites were about to be performed, as lawyers and officials passed to and fro wearing solemn and portentous expressions.

Rosa said nothing in response to Jane Crenlow's observation, but wondered, not for the first time, whether Mr Justice Ambrose had really been the intended target. The thought had first come to her as she listened to a late night news bulletin on the radio when the possibility of foul play had been mooted.

Not only did Judge Holtby look careworn, but Leo Dodd appeared to be equally ill at ease. She presumed that the police must already have interviewed both of them. On her own arrival at court that morning she had made it known to one of the investigating team that she had been a witness of what had happened and would be in court all day if required. The officer, Detective Sergeant Luke, had thanked her and said he would let his superiors know.

On a signal from the clerk of the court, Blaker and his co-defendants stepped into the dock. It was noticeable that Marcus Watt put distance between himself and the other three. There was a distinct air of tension when he was called upon to plead.

'Not guilty,' he said in a voice that trembled while his face glistened like a freshly-wet pavement.

Rosten, the junior prosecuting counsel, frowned and leaned across to whisper to David Pilly who was defending Watt.

'I thought your chap was going to plead guilty, David,' he said in a slightly accusing tone.

'I did warn you not to take anything for granted,' Pilly replied ruefully.

'Can't you have a word with him and get Leo Dodd to put the charge again?' Rosten said in a tone of irritation.

Pilly shook his head vigorously. 'Just be patient,' he replied.

David Pilly had been told by his instructing solicitor only a couple of minutes before the judge took his seat that their client was in a highly emotional and volatile state and, at that particular moment, was in greater fear of Bernard Blaker than of any opposing forces. Pilly had accepted the news philosophically and still thought it likely that Watt might change his plea in the course of the trial and be prepared to give evidence for the crown. The carrot dangling in front of his nose as an inducement to do so was the certainty of a lighter sentence than he might otherwise receive.

In the meantime, the jury was being sworn and soon Nicholas Barrow would be opening the case for the prosecution.

Bernard Blaker had shed his vicuna coat and had draped it over the back of his chair for on this the court's first working day, the latest device in air-conditioning was producing a temperature suitable to the tropics. He sat at the far end of the row from Watt, radiating an air of total calm and self-

20

assurance. He even managed to look cool.

Jane Crenlow and Paul Elson, with Rosa in attendance, had conferred with him briefly that morning, more out of courtesy than necessity. It had been a meeting which had served to reinforce Rosa's distaste for their client. The smoother and more urbane his manner, the more sinister he became.

Nicholas Barrow was not known for brevity and his opening speech to the jury was expected to last most of the morning as he took them through the details of the prosecution's evidence. From her place just behind her own two counsel, Rosa was able to observe the four defendants as well as Judge Holtby, who continued to look ill at ease and preoccupied. Rosa couldn't help wondering whether he was in a fit condition to try a complex case that was likely to throw up an abundance of thorny legal issues. He was obviously finding it hard to concentrate and kept on fidgeting in his chair.

'Poor chap must have a boil on his behind,' Paul Elson whispered to Rosa with a wink.

'Or something on his mind,' she murmured back.

Elson made a face and nodded.

Rosa glanced towards her client who was sitting back in his chair in the dock with arms folded across his chest and watching the judge with a thoughtful expression. After a while he slowly turned his head and put the jury under a lengthy scrutiny. Probably deciding which of them is open to being nobbled, Rosa reflected.

Prosecuting counsel had been addressing the jury for about twenty minutes when Detective Sergeant Luke tiptoed up to where Rosa was sitting.

'Detective Chief Superintendent Everson presents his compliments, Miss Epton, and wonders if you could conveniently slip out of court as he'd like to talk to you.'

Rosa leaned forward and whispered to Paul Elson, who nodded.

As she departed behind Sergeant Luke, she was aware of

21

the judge's gaze following her. Fortunately her client's attention seemed to be elsewhere and she scurried past the dock unnoticed.

'Mr Everson's set up a temporary headquarters in one of the administrator's rooms,' Sergeant Luke said as they got outside. 'One thing about these new courts, there's lots of space. This building actually gives the impression of having been designed by someone who knows what it's like to work in a court, which is more than you can say for most.'

He led the way down a floor and through a stout door marked 'private'. A thickly carpeted corridor stretched ahead. He knocked on a door on the left and opened it.

'Miss Epton, sir,' he announced, standing aside to let Rosa enter.

Chief Superintendent Everson was gazing out of the window at the swollen river whose muddy waters were only a few feet away.

'Hello, Miss Epton, sorry to get you out of court, but I felt it was a good idea to start my enquiries at the scene by talking to you. I gather you actually witnessed what happened?'

'Quite a lot of people must have.'

'But one likes to kick off with someone reliable,' he said with a smile. He took a final glance out of the window. 'It'll be a pity if the next bit of drama is flood water all over this expensive carpeting,' he added in a mordant tone.

'I doubt if the river will rise that much.'

'Let's hope not! A judge swept away and drowned is enough to be getting on with.' He fixed her with a steady look. 'I'd be grateful if you'd tell me exactly what you saw. Incidentally this room is directly beneath the one where the buffet was held.' He pointed out of the window. 'And that overhang is the balcony above. From what I've been told so far, Mr Justice Ambrose must have fallen backwards into the river opposite this very window.'

Rosa stared across at the bank on the farther side and nodded.

'Yes, I think that's near enough right.'

22

'Let's sit down and you tell me what happened. We can get it down in statement form later. Just before you begin, let me ask you this, did you know the judge personally?'

'No.'

'What about Judge Holtby and Judge Welford?'

'I've had cases in front of both when they were sitting at other courts.'

'And?'

'And what?'

'What's your view of them?'

'Is that relevant to Mr Justice Ambrose's death?' Rosa enquired.

Everson ran a hand across his close-cropped grizzled head and gave a shrug.

'Probably not, but I'd still be interested in your answer if you're prepared to give me one. In confidence, of course.'

'They're both competent without being spectacular.'

'It's hardly for a humble policeman to say so, but I'd have thought spectacular judges were something of a hazard.'

Rosa smiled. There wasn't much of the humble policeman about Detective Chief Superintendent Everson. He was a tough officer of the old school if ever she saw one.

'I'm sure you're right,' she said. 'That's why spectacular advocates don't usually make good judges.'

'Do you know either of these two personally?'

'I've met Judge Holtby socially. He and his wife were at a party I went to last Christmas.'

'I'm told he's quite a party-goer.'

'He certainly gave every appearance of enjoying himself.'

'Did you speak to his wife at yesterday's ceremony?'

'I didn't see her. As a matter of fact I don't think either she or Judge Welford's wife were here.'

Everson gave a slow nod of comprehension. 'I expect discretion kept them away. I gather that Mrs Welford was once Lady Ambrose.'

'Yes.'

'In that case her presence would obviously have been an

embarrassment all round.'

'To put it mildly.'

'You think that Mrs Holtby stayed away to make Mrs Welford's absence appear less pointed?'

'That would be my guess.'

'Mine, too. But now let's get down to the real nitty gritty of what happened out on that balcony . . .'

Everson listened closely as Rosa described what she had seen. When she had finished, he said, 'You didn't actually see any wound in the judge's neck?'

'No.'

'What did you think had caused him to fall backwards?'

'I had no idea. As I've said, his hand flew up to his neck and the next moment he'd gone.'

'Do you attach any significance to the slight gap you've described between Judge Holtby and Mr Justice Ambrose on his right?'

'Not really. I'm sure it had an innocent explanation. And it wasn't all that much of a gap.'

'The people taking photographs were all on your right, as I understand it?'

'Yes. More or less in the same line as myself.'

'How many of them would you say?'

'About eight or ten.'

'It seems there were only two official photographers. One freelance and one from a local paper. The rest were presumably family and friends.'

'The one closest to me was a boy of about twelve.'

'That was probably Mr Dodd's son. Needless to say I'm anxious to identify everyone who was out on the balcony at the time.'

'There's a rumour that somebody fired a poison pellet from a camera,' Rosa remarked.

'For once rumour is spot on,' he said grimly.

She gave a small shiver and frowned as she again tried to visualise the scene. But all that floated before her mind's eye was a kaleidoscope of people holding cameras in front of their

24

faces. She could recall a young man with long hair who was wearing a leather jacket and whom she took, from the quantity of equipment slung round his neck, to be one of the professionals. Also a moist-faced woman in a garden party hat who was clearly someone's wife. And, of course, the boy closest to her who was apparently Leo Dodd's son. The rest remained just a blur. She couldn't even say what sex they were. She prided herself on her observation and it irked her that she was unable to recall more. But then she wasn't to know what was going to happen.

'I expect you want to get back to your case, Miss Epton,' Everson said, breaking in on her thoughts. 'Should anything further occur to you, please let me know immediately. As you'll now realise, you were standing very close to a murderer on that balcony. A murderer who was armed with an extremely sophisticated weapon and who showed skill and determination in carrying out his crime.'

'Has it occurred to you, Mr Everson, that he may nevertheless have killed the wrong person?'

Everson gave her a long thoughtful stare before replying. 'No, it hadn't,' he said slowly. 'But I shall bear it in mind.'

Chapter 5

Denise Holtby felt on edge that morning. She knew her husband was worried and that always upset her. And to crown matters her son, Ian, was still in bed at eleven o'clock.

She had on an emerald green silk blouse and a pair of tailored black slacks. Being small and slim she was able to look good in clothes that many women her age were better advised not to wear. Moreover, she was still a natural blonde.

She often wished she had a pound note for every time someone exclaimed, 'I can't believe you have four grown-up children.' To which she would invariably reply in her almost accent-free English, 'Just three and a half are grown up. Paul's only fourteen.'

When the telephone rang, she hurried into the hall to answer it.

'Denise? It's Heather Welford.'

'*Chérie*, I was just about to call you,' she said quickly. 'I wanted to phone last night, but Tony said I wasn't to worry you. My dear, what can I say? It's been a terrible shock to all of us, but to you in particular, even though you were no longer married to Edmund. And poor Stephen! He must be feeling dreadful, too.'

'I still can't really believe it's happened,' Heather Welford said, as Denise paused to draw breath.

'I'm so thankful that you and I weren't there,' Denise burst out. 'Tony's devastated and I'm sure Stephen is, too.'

'As you know, Stephen and Edmund were hardly on speaking terms and Stephen was furious when he learnt that

26

Edmund was coming as the visiting High Court judge. He believed he had done it on purpose to embarrass him. It would have been typical of Edmund to do a thing like that.'

'How you must have suffered when you were married to him!' Denise remarked with a throb in her voice. 'And how romantic when you ran away with Stephen, the handsomest judge in the land! It shows what everyone thought of Edmund that Stephen was able to ride the *scandale* and remain a judge.'

'Only just,' Heather observed with a nervous laugh. *Scandale*, she noted, was one of half a dozen words that Denise still determinedly pronounced in the French way. She now went on, 'What I was really ringing to ask you, Denise, was whether the police have been to see you yet?'

'Why should they want to see me, *chérie*? I can't tell them anything when I wasn't there.'

'Stephen believes they'll want to interview both of us. Hasn't Tony said that, too?'

'No. But he's always told me never to speak to the police about anything without letting him know first.'

Heather Welford thought this was probably sound husbandly advice given Denise's tendency to talk too much. It was not that she was stupid. On the contrary she had a sharp mind and could show great shrewdness, but she had the gallic trait of volubility.

Denise now went on, 'But what can we tell the police if we weren't there?'

'They may be after background,' Heather said vaguely.

'It's crazy. I shall refuse to speak to them,' Denise said excitedly.

'They're much more likely to want to see me than you. I mean, I am Edmund's ex-wife.'

'But it is three years since the divorce and you have not seen him since, eh?'

'That's true.'

'Then what can you possibly tell them?'

'I don't really know, save that motives for murder often

27

originate in the past.'

'But that's absurd where you are concerned.'

'It's Stephen I'm worried about. He survived the original scandal only to get involved in this.'

'But he is not, as you put it, involved. He did not murder Edmund. He and Tony were standing there together while the photographs were being taken. Tony has told me exactly how it was.'

'I realise all that, Denise, but can't you see what the newspapers are going to make of it? There'll be enough innuendo to force Stephen to resign.'

'Poof to the newspapers and their lies! Of course Stephen won't have to resign.'

'If *everything* came out, he'd have to,' Heather said bleakly.

'What do you mean, *chérie*?' Denise asked in a puzzled voice.

'It was just after I had left Edmund. Stephen was so indignant at the way he had treated me that he wrote him a letter. Give me your word, Denise, that you'll never tell Stephen I've mentioned this. Not even Tony . . .'

'I am crossing my heart now.'

'In the letter he said that unless Edmund agreed to a quiet divorce, he wouldn't hesitate to let the legal world know just how badly he had treated me.'

'But why shouldn't he say that? Stephen has always been a gentleman.'

'It wasn't a gentleman's letter. It was more that of a blackmailer.'

'And what was Edmund's reaction?'

'The divorce went through quietly.'

'It shows Edmund had cause to fear for his own reputation. It would have been he who would have had to resign as a judge if the truth had come out.'

'The point is, where is that letter?'

'He probably threw it away in a rage.'

'Not Edmund. He would have kept it. He was totally

28

unforgiving to those who crossed him.'

'But he has never tried to make trouble for Stephen, has he?'

'No, but that doesn't mean he wasn't biding his time. The fact that he particularly asked to be the first visiting High Court judge at Runnymede Crown Court could have been a move towards revenge. He knew Stephen had been appointed one of the permanent judges at the court and yet he applied to come. As one of the senior Queen's Bench judges he can usually pick and choose where he'll go.'

'You mustn't worry, *chérie*, I'm sure he did destroy that letter. And even if he didn't, the contents may never become known. Edmund has gone, he cannot touch your lives any more.'

'I wish I could believe that,' Heather Welford said bleakly.

'Have courage! Cherish your Stephen as I try and cherish my Tony,' Denise exclaimed theatrically.

Heather gave a small laugh.

'I know, Denise, what a devoted wife and mother you are. Incidentally, how are the children?'

'Only Ian is at home. Charles is at technical college and Susan and Paul are at school. We have Paul at weekends.'

'Ian's all right, is he?' The question was prompted by her knowledge that Denise's son by her first marriage had been something of a problem child. Since leaving school early he had drifted from one casual employment to another, always returning home when the pressure of life became too much for him.

'Yes, he is fine,' Denise said stoutly. 'He's so helpful to me when he's at home,' she added untruthfully.

Their conversation ended shortly afterwards and she went upstairs to find out if her son was getting up. Opening his door she peered across at the bed. Only the top of his head was visible and she went and pulled back the duvet. A bleary eye looked up at her.

'Brought me a cup of tea?' he murmured thickly.

'No, you must get up.'

29

'I've nothing to get up for. Why can't I stay here where I'm out of everyone's way?'

'It's not good for you lying in bed all day. It's demoralising.'

He rolled over on to his back and stared mournfully up at his mother.

'I'm not going out, so why can't I stay in bed? Anyway, I'm tired.'

'You're always tired.'

'I know. It's because I'm depressed.' He stretched out a warm hand and she took it in one of hers. 'You must sometimes wish I'd never been born, mum.'

She gave his hand a squeeze. 'Now you are just feeling sorry for yourself.'

'I'm also sorry for all the trouble I cause. I mean that.'

'I know you are, my darling. That's why I help you.'

'You help me because you love me. I've always known that you really love me more than the others. I suppose it's because I'm your first-born and because I've never known my father. It's true, isn't it, that you do love me the most?'

'I love you, my darling,' Denise said with a slight break in her voice, 'because you've always needed my protection.' After a pause she murmured, 'Get up and I'll cook you some breakfast.'

'I just want a cup of tea. I couldn't eat a thing.'

'Get up, anyway!'

'I wish I could sleep for ever.'

'There'll be time for that when you die. But that's not going to happen yet, so get up!'

He gave his mother a suspicious stare. 'What do you know that I don't?' he asked.

'A great many things, I hope. Now get up!'

'No, seriously, mum. You're hiding something from me, aren't you?'

'Get up! Get up!' she repeated as she walked briskly out of the room.

30

Chapter 6

Henry Keffingham had not looked forward to appearing in front of Mr Justice Ambrose in a complex drugs case. He had always regarded the judge as a prig and a hypocrite.

Keffingham himself was an effective advocate whose weakness was to allow his desire to win a case to overcome his moral scruples on occasions. For him the barrister's ethical code of practice was something to be fenced with and skated around when necessary, which was another way of saying that he would invariably pull a fast one if he thought he could get away with it.

It was this propensity that had landed him in trouble with Ambrose, J. only a few weeks before the opening of Runnymede Crown Court. It had been a civil case, in which by sleight of hand, or rather sleight of advocacy, he had misled the judge about the status of a vital witness he was calling. When the truth subsequently slipped out, Ambrose, J. had been furious and an alarmed Henry Keffingham had hurried round to see him in his room when the court rose and had put the best gloss he could on his conduct. The judge had severely castigated him and had said he would consider reporting him to the benchers of his Inn for professional misconduct. Each of them was aware that any such action must damage Keffingham's practice.

In the event, Mr Justice Ambrose had not taken this drastic step, but had mentioned the matter to his clerk, who had told Leo Dodd when discussing the judge's list with him a week before the new court's opening. Leo Dodd had passed the

31

word on to his deputy as an item of professional gossip and he, in turn, had told Detective Chief Superintendent Everson.

It was later when speaking on the telephone to Dodd himself about the arrangements for the opening ceremony that Ambrose, J. had flayed the unfortunate clerk and told him he was not fit for his job. His deputy had been present in the room at the time and had also passed this on to Everson. Hence Everson's feeling that motives were being laid at his feet like bones brought into the house by a faithful hound.

But to get back to Henry Keffingham. He was now certain that the trial would go his way and that Gail Bristow would be acquitted. He reckoned he could tie Tony Holtby in such knots that fear of strictures by the Court of Appeal would ensure his summing-up for a verdict of not guilty. In fact, with the judge in his present mood, it was going to be hard not to over-exploit the situation. Ambrose, J.'s demise was undoubtedly an undisguised blessing for all the defending counsel and Henry Keffingham made no effort to pretend otherwise.

He sat back and gazed along the row at Nicholas Barrow, who was still addressing the jury and showing every sign of doing so for the rest of the day. It was incredible how long-winded some of his colleagues could be. Their advocacy had all the finesse of a steam-roller. He glanced over his shoulder at his client in the dock. She had elegance and finesse all right. A damn pretty girl with auburn hair tumbling round her shoulders and the clear, pale green eyes of a cat. He understood she was Blaker's current mistress, which said much for his good taste. Keffingham also awarded him points for having Jane Crenlow as his defending counsel. She was as able as they came and way ahead of all the other counsel in the case – apart from himself, of course.

He turned his attention once more to the judge who was hunched in his seat as if succumbing to a dose of 'flu. Old Ambrose's death really had knocked him for six. Anyone might think he was involved in some way, whereas only twenty-four hours before he had been out on that balcony

32

without an apparent care.

Keffingham had flatly refused to join the VIPs lined up in front of the array of cameras. The last thing he had wanted was to be seen in that company.

He stared up at the ceiling and yawned. Was Nicholas Barrow never going to sit down?

Much the same thought was passing through Leo Dodd's mind as he sat at his desk immediately below the judge's dais. He had always maintained that a clerk of the court required tact, inexhaustible patience and an ability to have one ear open to what was going on around him while giving a large part of his mind to paperwork which would otherwise pile up on his office desk.

But today he was in no mood to attend to any of the correspondence he had brought with him into court, nor yet to sit back and listen to prosecuting counsel opening his case to the jury. At the best of times listening to Nicholas Barrow was akin to munching dry biscuits. The more you chewed, the less able you were to swallow. He had always been an advocate to make his colleagues' hearts sink every time he rose to his feet. Leo Dodd couldn't help reflecting that Mr Justice Ambrose would have been showing considerable impatience long before now, had he been trying the case. But Tony Holtby would let counsel drone on uninterrupted. He had already told Dodd that he intended to let the case try itself.

The clerk of the court had gone along to the judge's room half an hour before the court sat and they had discussed the previous day's events.

'I must say, Leo,' Holtby had said, 'the last thing I feel like doing is trying this drugs case. All those defence counsel waiting to trip me up if I don't fall over my own feet first.'

'I'm sure Stephen Welford would take the case into his list . . .'

'No, no. It's an important case and as senior judge, I should try it. It's just that I've not yet got over the shock of yesterday, but I'll cope. As you know, I'd read the depositions before Ambrose decided he wanted to take it and it's not as

33

evidentially intricate as it might be. Much will depend on whether the alleged confessions are admissible.' He let out a sigh. 'I suppose the officers investigating Ambrose's death will be around the building for several days. I just hope they comport themselves discreetly. One obviously can't refuse them reasonable facilities or deny them an interview, but I hope they wear their carpet slippers and not their hob-nail boots.' He sighed again. 'What an inauspicious start to our new court!'

Leo Dodd had agreed and had left Judge Holtby staring out of his window at the scurrying river below. He personally regarded it as not so much inauspicious as disastrous. He had been delighted when he was offered the job. A brand new court in an agreeable area and two permanent judges with whom he reckoned to get along without difficulty, for both Tony Holtby and Stephen Welford were men of his own sort. Each was as free of judicial quirks as could be hoped for.

The first blow had come when Ambrose, J. had quite gratuitously rebuked him on the telephone and, in the most unpleasant manner, had questioned his ability to perform his duties properly.

This had greatly upset him; alarmed him, too, for heaven alone knew to whom he mightn't repeat his unfair judgement. Leo Dodd was a long way off retirement and hoped for future advancement in his career, but a High Court judge making critical observations about you was scarcely a recommendation to the powers that be.

His determined and ambitious wife, Eileen, had been furious when he told her.

'I'll wring his scrawny neck if I ever get the chance,' she had said indignantly. 'He'd better watch out if I ever meet him.'

She never had met him, but she had been at the opening ceremony and had taken her camera.

He recalled having said to her that morning with a nervous laugh, for she was still burning with anger on his behalf, 'Bring your camera, darling, but better leave your revolver behind!'

34

Chapter 7

The appeal by the police to everyone who had taken photographs to come forward and bring their cameras with them produced, in the first instance, nine telephone calls.

Detective Inspector Martin was assigned to this aspect of the enquiry and by the end of the next day had interviewed all those concerned. With the assistance of a member of Scotland Yard's photographic branch he had also examined their cameras. None of them turned out to be a lethal weapon in disguise.

'I wasn't expecting the murderer to step forward and show us how he did it,' Everson remarked when Martin reported to him.

By this time Everson also knew that the pathologist had excised a tiny pellet from Mr Justice Ambrose's neck which was embedded in the skin just below the angle of his jaw on the right side. It was only a sixteenth of an inch in diameter and was made of a platinum-iridium alloy. It had two microscopic holes in it and laboratory examination was expected to reveal the nature of any poison it contained. If it proved to be ricin, the poison fatally injected into the Bulgarian defector, Markov, Everson assumed it would as surely have led to the death of Mr Justice Ambrose, had he not drowned first.

'So we've traced nine photographers,' Everson now said. 'Is that the lot?'

'There were certainly ten,' Martin replied, 'because Mrs Dodd spoke for her son as well as herself. There could have

35

been as many as twelve.'

'Explain!'

'I gather there was a good deal of jostling out on the balcony with people trying to get in good positions, so that there was never any actual count of numbers. It's possible there were others who, for one reason or another, haven't come forward.'

'But only one of them is a murderer. Have you checked and cross-checked who was next to who?'

Martin nodded. 'The two professionals were next to each other in the centre. Adrian Burt from the *Gazette* and Gary Lewis who's a freelance. Burt remembers a large formidable woman on his left who must have been Mrs Dodd. He remembers her because she stuck her elbow into him just as he was about to take a picture and he gave her a bit of his mind. Mrs Dodd recalls a girl of about twenty on her other side and that was Caroline Turner, whose father is the taxing officer at the court. Next to her was another girl, Debbie Richards, whose boyfriend is a clerk in the general office. She says she thinks there was someone on her left but she can't be sure as she was busily concentrating on what she was doing. It was her boyfriend's camera and she was scared of pressing the wrong button. It could have been Mr Dodd's son . . .'

Everson nodded. 'Miss Epton remembers a boy next to her.'

Martin consulted the piece of paper he was holding. 'Going the other way, Gary Lewis remembers a woman next to him whom he describes as being a bit overdressed. She turns out to be Mrs Pitt, the janitor's wife. Next to her was a youth I've not yet been able to trace . . .'

'You mean that no youth fitting his description has come forward?' Everson asked sharply.

'I haven't really got a description, sir. Mrs Pitt just recalls seeing a youth out of the corner of her eye. He was slim and had dark hair and she doesn't remember seeing him again afterwards.'

'What about the person on the further side? Does he or she

36

remember this youth?'

'No, that was Judge Welford's brother and he says he vaguely recalls somebody pushing between himself and Mrs Pitt.'

'Surely he can do better than that,' Everson said with a frown.

'I'm afraid not, sir. He recently suffered a stroke which has left him partially paralysed. It's also affected his sight on that side.'

'But he was still able to use a camera!' Everson observed. 'Anyone else unaccounted for?'

'Somebody called Nigel Ambrose,' Martin said, with the air of a conjuror producing a final rabbit from his hat.

'Ambrose, did you say?'

'Yes, sir. A nephew of the judge and a bit of a ne'er-do-well from what I've been able to gather. Unfortunately, I've not yet been able to trace him. He was recently living at a bed and breakfast place in Earls Court, but he left there the day before yesterday and hasn't been back.'

'That would be the day of the opening ceremony?'

Martin nodded. 'It's obviously important that we find him as soon as possible.'

'If he's not been traced, how do you know he was there? Did somebody recognise him?'

'Yes. By pure chance he was spotted by one of the catering staff who had once worked with him behind the bar of a public house. I say by pure chance, sir, because I've checked that he wasn't on the list of invited guests.'

'So he was a gatecrasher.'

'Yes.'

'He doesn't sound the sort of person who'd be taking photos for his family album, so what was he doing there?'

'Exactly, sir. What?'

Everson was quiet for a while. Then he said in a decisive tone, 'We must concentrate on finding him and also on tracing the youth who hasn't come forward. I would think we can quickly eliminate the two professional photographers,

37

also Mrs Dodd and her son and the various girls you've mentioned. Moreover, Judge Welford's brother doesn't seem a very likely suspect in the circumstances.'

'There's one odd detail about him that I've not yet cleared up, sir. Mrs Pitt is sure he had two cameras round his neck. He's handed in only one to the police and denies possessing a second.'

'So what's the explanation?'

'Mrs Pitt still feels certain he had two.'

'I can see you have a theory,' Everson said with a touch of impatience. 'Out with it!'

'He has a deaf aid. One of those old-fashioned sorts which is pinned to his chest and could be mistaken for a camera.'

'I thought they went out years ago. Have you examined it?'

'Yes, sir. It's genuine enough.'

'Are you suggesting he has a second identical one that fires poison pellets?'

Inspector Martin shrugged. 'Nothing's too fanciful or bizarre in this case, is it, sir?'

Everson gave a grunt. 'We'd better keep Judge Welford's brother in mind after all as a suspect.' He scratched his chest through an unbuttoned gap in his shirt. 'I think we might pay a visit to Mrs Welford and see what she can tell us about her ex-husband and his nephew, not to mention her brother-in-law. If we go now, we'll catch her before her husband gets home.' With a sardonic gleam in his eye, he added, 'That's always an advantage when interviewing wives. Incidentally, when will all these films be developed?'

'It's being done now. Fortunately nobody made a fuss about handing theirs over.'

'I should hope not.'

'I told them we'd probably supply better prints than any shop, and free at that.'

'Don't let the Receiver discover that or you'll find your next pay packet docked.'

Martin grinned. 'It'll be worth it if one of the photos solves the case for us.'

'About as likely as your becoming the next Commissioner!'

'I'm pinning a lot of hope on those photographs, sir,' Martin said staunchly.

'I'll certainly be interested in noting the expressions on people's faces. If anyone's registering shock or surprise, I'll want to know why. By the way, nobody's to see them until I say so. I don't want the whole world looking at them until I've assessed their value.'

'They're going to provide valuable evidence, sir. I feel it in my water.'

'There's enough water in this case without yours. We may yet all end up in an ark.'

Chapter 8

When the car pulled up outside, Heather Welford was standing irresolutely in the front room that her husband used as a study.

She could see the tops of two heads above the thick beech hedge that screened the house from the road and a moment later two men came into view as they pushed open the wooden gate and advanced up the path.

She knew at once they were police officers. Indeed, it never entered her head they could be anything else. It wasn't the way they were dressed, but the manner in which they glanced about them as if they had just undergone a course in observation.

The Welfords lived in a pleasant modern house set in about half an acre of garden in one of Surrey's so-called stockbroker belts. It was only twenty minutes' drive from the new Crown Court, which was why Stephen Welford had applied to be posted there.

'The lady at the window has disappeared,' Martin murmured as they reached the front door.

'Probably gone to repair her face for male visitors,' Everson remarked, as he rang the bell.

A few seconds later they heard footsteps inside and the door was opened.

'Mrs Welford?' Everson enquired politely.

'Yes.' She sounded nervous.

'I'm Detective Chief Superintendent Everson and this is my colleague, Detective Inspector Martin. I'm in charge of

the investigation into the death of Mr Justice Ambrose. May
we come in?'
'Yes. I'm afraid you'll find the place in a bit of a muddle. I
didn't get any housework done this morning and so I'd just
begun when you arrived. We'd better go into the drawing-
room.' She led the way into a bright, cheerful room which
had long windows looking on to a lawn. 'Sit where you like.
Shall I make some tea?'

Everson shook his head. 'Not for us, Mrs Welford,' he
said firmly. Martin let out an imperceptible sigh. He was
ready for a cup of tea any hour of the day and, given half a
chance, had never been known to refuse the offer.

'May I begin by asking you some background questions?'
Everson went on. 'I understand you were once married to Mr
Justice Ambrose?'

'Yes.'

'For how long?'

'Twenty-two years.'

'Do you have any children by that marriage?'

'No.'

'Nor by your present marriage?'

'I was forty-six when I married Stephen,' she said with a
faint smile.

'When was that?'

'About two and a half years ago.'

'What were the grounds for the divorce?'

'Sir Edmund Ambrose divorced me. The usual grounds.
Adultery.' She paused and gazed down at the plain gold ring
on her wedding finger. 'I could have petitioned for divorce
on the grounds of my first husband's cruelty. It would have
meant, however, washing a lot of very dirty linen in public
and causing untold hurt to a number of innocent people. It
was simpler to let him institute the proceedings.'

'And you married Judge Welford as soon as the divorce
was through?'

'Yes. We had been living together from the time I ran away
from my first husband.'

'What sort of man was Sir Edmund?' Everson asked mildly.

She leaned forward on the edge of her chair. 'I imagine you've heard a lot of things about him. Probably all nasty. Well, multiply them by ten and you're approaching a true picture. He was a cold, cruel, sadistic monster. I don't mean physically, but intellectually.' She gave them a quick glance. 'You're doubtless wondering why I ever married him? The answer is that I was an innocent twenty-two-year-old who was totally starry-eyed over this brilliant young barrister. I was flattered that he deigned to speak to me and seek my company.' She paused and stared pensively at the carpet. 'And now you're wondering why I stayed with him for twenty-two years? And the answer to that is that I didn't have much alternative. I had no independent means of support and whenever I threatened to leave him he would either go into a cold rage or he'd apply emotional blackmail. I had nobody to whom I could turn. Both my parents had died while I was still at school and I didn't have any brothers or sisters.'

'It sounds like life in hell,' Everson remarked quietly.

'It was.'

After a pause he said, 'I understand you didn't attend the opening of Runnymede Crown Court the day before yesterday?'

'That's not very surprising, is it, in view of what I've told you?'

'Did Mrs Holtby stay away so as to make your absence less obvious?'

'Yes. My husband had a word with Judge Holtby. Later I spoke to Mrs Holtby myself on the phone and thanked her.'

'I believe Judge Welford's brother attended?'

'Poor Barney; yes, he had my ticket. He had a stroke about a year ago which has left him considerably disabled, but he was thrilled to go.'

'Did he know your ex-husband?'

'What, Barney know Edmund? It was through Barney

42

that I came to meet Stephen. He was a very clever book-binder and was particularly skilled at restoring old volumes that were falling apart. He was recommended to Edmund, who engaged him to renovate a collection of Shakespeare and another of Milton that had belonged to his great grandfather. We were living in Addison Road at the time and Barney came to the house. Because Edmund made such a fuss about the books being taken away, Barney agreed to work there, provided he was given the facilities and provided, also, that Edmund recompensed him for shutting up his own shop during the period. I may say that Edmund was outraged by the suggestion, but had to give in if he wanted the job done. In the event, Barney spent the best part of four weeks working at the house and I naturally got to know him rather well. He had told me he had a younger brother who was a barrister and whom he would like me to meet. And so it came about.'

Everson had the impression that she had wanted to give a quick, factual gloss to the episode involving her meeting Barney Welford and his restoration of her husband's precious volumes of Shakespeare and Milton. Everson himself had the merest acquaintance with Shakespeare and would never have heard of Milton, had his daughter on one occasion not referred to him as an old drear. The poet that is, not her father. As a result he had picked up the volume she was studying for her A-level English and begun reading Paradise Lost. It had not taken him long to agree with her judgement. It now occurred to him that Milton and Mr Justice Ambrose were two of a kind.

Heather Welford now went on. 'After Barney had completed the work, Edmund carped at the price and tried to make out that the job hadn't been done to specification. Barney was very upset, but knocked a hundred pounds off his bill rather than face a long drawn-out argument.'

'Did he bear any ill-will against Sir Edmund?'

'Practically everyone who had any dealings with Edmund was left bearing him ill-will.'

'Why was Barney so pleased to be invited to attend the

43

opening of the Court?'

'Because of Stephen. They've always been close and Barney's immensely proud of his younger brother's achievement in becoming a judge. Even the prospect of seeing Edmund didn't deter him. He had no intention of speaking to him anyway.'

A silence fell during which each seemed to be occupied with his own thoughts. Eventually, Everson said, 'I take it you know who Nigel Ambrose is?'

She gave him a startled look.

'He's Edmund's nephew,' she said warily.

'What can you tell me about him?'

'Don't say he's popped up in this affair!'

'That remains to be seen. Do you know where I can get in touch with him?'

She shook her head. 'I've no idea. He drifts from one address to another and I've not had any contact with him since my divorce. Well, virtually not. He did write to me about a year ago asking if I could lend him some money and I wrote back saying I couldn't.'

'Where was he living then?'

'In the Kilburn area. I don't recall the actual address and I tore up his letter as soon as I'd answered it.'

'Tell me more about him.'

'He must be in his early forties now. Edmund had one sister, a few years older than himself. She married an absolute rogue and died giving birth to Nigel, who was brought up by his father. Except that brought up is scarcely the right expression. He was dragged from pillar to post until he was old enough to stand on his own two feet. At the same time he assumed his mother's maiden name. Not that that seems to have helped him and he's been constantly in and out of trouble.'

'Prison, do you mean?'

'Not as far as I know, though I imagine that's more due to good fortune than anything else. From time to time he'd pop up in our lives when I was married to Edmund, invariably

44

asking for help. Money.'

'Used hc to get it?'

'Occasionally at the beginning. Edmund had been very fond of his sister. Possibly the only person he ever was fond of and so he was prepared to help Nigel for her sake, but that didn't last long. Once he realised what a feckless and irresponsible person he was, he quickly hardened his heart and refused him further assistance. From time to time Nigel would phone or turn up on the doorstep only to receive the coldest possible reception from his Uncle Edmund. Once or twice he tried to get me to intercede, but little did he know what a futile hope that was!'

'Did you like him?'

'Like?' she repeated in a reflective tone. 'Sometimes I felt sorry for him. I think I even understood him. After all we were not that far apart in age. But I can't say I liked him. The trouble was one couldn't trust him.'

'He gate-crashed the opening of the Court two days ago,' Everson said. 'Can you suggest any reason for his doing so?'

She blinked in surprise. 'Absolutely not! Of course I've no idea what his relationship with Edmund has been since our divorce.'

'A reconciliation hardly seems likely from all you've said.'

'I agree. Most unlikely.'

'So assuming he's remained on bad terms with his uncle, what do you imagine would have been his motive in attending the ceremony?'

'Did somebody recognise him?' Everson nodded and after an interval she said, 'I've really no idea why he should have been there.'

'Had he ever, to your knowledge, threatened Sir Edmund with violence?'

'No . . . not seriously,' she murmured.

'What do you mean by *seriously*?'

'He never threatened to kill him or harm him or anything like that. Once or twice he wrote blustering letters saying that Edmund would one day pay for having refused him help. What he meant, I'm sure, was that it would lie on Edmund's conscience. But, as I say, I've no idea what contact they've had in the past couple of years.'

'Do you happen to know whether Nigel was a photographer?'

'Not as far as I know. I never saw him with a camera.'

'Well, we must try and find him and discover what he was doing at the court's opening,' Everson remarked.

'I'm sure there's an innocent explanation.'

Everson shot her a sceptical look. He wondered why she felt it necessary to make such a glib observation.

'I mean, there usually is for most things, isn't there?' she added in a slightly embarrassed voice.

'Innocent explanations don't always live up to their appearance: at least, not in murder investigations,' Everson replied.

Suddenly the telephone started to ring and she glanced about her, as if trapped. There was an instrument on a small table beside the fireplace and almost certainly extensions in other parts of the house. It was apparent that she was torn with indecision as to where to take the call. After an awkward pause she got up and walked over to the phone in the room while Everson and Martin assumed expressions of innocent unconcern.

'Oh, hello, darling . . . well, actually they're here . . . yes, at this moment,' she said as her two visitors exchanged a swift look. 'It's Detective Chief Superintendent Everson and Detective Inspector Martin . . . We're all in the drawing-room,' she added quickly. 'They've been asking me about Edmund . . . No, I'm fine . . . nothing wrong at all . . . I'll tell you everything when you get back . . . No, of course I won't . . . goodbye, darling.'

She dropped the receiver as though it had begun to scorch her hand.

"Of course I won't" what? Everson wondered. Say too much, his mind supplied.

'That was my husband,' she said unnecessarily as she returned to her chair. 'A juror in the case he was trying has

46

been taken ill, so he's adjourned early.' She paused and then said earnestly, 'I can't tell you how upset he is over what's happened.' She gave a short nervous laugh. 'We're both worried about each other, but I suppose that's natural. It couldn't be a more embarrassing situation and the gutter press is bound to exploit it for all it's worth. They'll probably sell thousands of extra copies of their trashy papers.' She shivered and stared abstractedly at the tirelessly leaping flames of the simulated coal fire.

Everson got up. 'Thank you for giving us your time, Mrs Welford. It's been a very helpful interview.'

'Will you be seeing my husband, too?'

'I'm sure we shall. I'll get in touch with him at the court.'

'There is just one thing . . .'

'Yes?'

'If you feel it necessary to interview his brother, Barney, don't be rough with him. He's not a fit person and he gets emotionally upset rather easily. It's the result of his stroke.'

'I'll remember that.'

'Thank you. Don't think I'm trying to interfere in your work, but I thought I should mention it.'

'I hope you haven't felt we were rough with you,' Everson remarked drily.

'Good gracious, no.'

'What did you make of her, sir?' Martin asked when they were back in the car.

'I think she told us the truth. But was it the whole truth?' Everson said slowly.

'Who on earth ever tells the police the whole truth?'

'If they don't, it's at their peril.'

'Trouble is, they're often in greater peril if they do.'

'You can stuff that fancy talk. I still belong to the school that believes cleanliness is next to godliness and that truth is a virtue and that virtue is its own reward. And don't try and cap that!'

'Back to Runnymede Court, sir?' Martin enquired sweetly.

'Yes, and let's hope those photographs are ready.'

47

Chapter 9

The second day of the trial had dragged even more than the first and Rosa had, at times, found it hard to conceal her boredom.

She had always disliked drugs cases. They were liable to produce arid legal arguments on the construction of the various regulations governing them which did nothing to engage her interest. The evidence was, for the most part, that of police and customs officers and usually involved details of lengthy interviews with defendants who invariably denied what they were alleged to have said. The ensuing contest was often that of the irresistible force meeting the immovable object. And lastly she rarely felt much sympathy for her clients who became enmeshed in this form of criminal activity.

As a lawyer she was not obliged to believe in a client's innocence, but it did help if you could identify with him or her as a fellow human being in some way. Certainly she and Bernard Blaker had nothing in common. They moved in entirely different worlds, social and financial.

From time to time as the day wore on she would cast him a covert glance as he sat impassively in the dock. It was impossible to guess what he was thinking. As yet the evidence had barely touched him and Jane Crenlow had done little cross-examination. She had the wisdom to let well alone and not stir the water unless she was quite certain what would appear when the mud had settled.

Henry Keffingham, on the other hand, had had a field day

cross-examining a stubborn but not very quick-witted customs officer who had given evidence of alleged admissions made to him by Gail Bristow. He revelled in the pyrotechnics of forensic advocacy and felt his fellow counsel should be grateful to him for injecting a bit of life into the proceedings.

The judge continued to look worn and distracted and to play an entirely passive role. Fortunately he had been required to give few rulings, but when he was appealed to by one side or the other, the effort of decision revealed itself in a certain tetchiness.

When the court adjourned for the day, Rosa waited to have a word with her client.

'I'm afraid it's going painfully slowly,' she said with a deprecating smile as they stood in a corner of the entrance hall.

He gave a resigned shrug. 'Once or twice I've wondered why I'm sitting there at all.'

'As you know, you're mainly implicated by the evidence of Detective Inspector Dawkin and he's still to be called.'

'A corrupt and lying officer, I'm afraid,' he remarked austerely. 'I suppose the crunch for me will come tomorrow.'

'Or the day after. The case might have taken various short cuts, but it doesn't seem that the judge is putting anyone under pressure to shorten matters.'

'Let justice be seen to be done, eh?' he remarked with a note of irony. After a pause he added, 'As long as it *is* done and we're found not guilty, I'm not complaining.'

Rosa decided that silence was the only reply to this. Soon afterwards they parted out in the car park where Blaker's chauffeur-driven Mercedes awaited. She hoped for his sake that none of the jurors fighting to get on buses witnessed his departure.

When she got back to London she found a note on her desk saying that a man had called and was most anxious to speak to her. He had phoned a second time only a few minutes before her return and would try again later. He had refused to leave his name. She pushed the note aside and gazed without much enthusiasm at the pile of papers awaiting her attention. She would obviously have to take most of them to work on at home that evening.

Home was a flat on Campden Hill where she had lived since first moving to London. Though tiny, it was the most relaxing place she knew and she never failed to feel soothed every time she let herself in through its front door, however late the hour and whatever her state of tiredness. It was a sanctuary and a refuge, even though her privacy was not infrequently invaded by telephone calls from people in trouble who had somehow managed to get hold of her home number. The number was now ex-directory and she had even thought of having it changed, but had been deterred by the thought of having to inform all her friends.

The phone on her desk rang and she reached for the receiver.

'It's the same man I left you a note about,' Stephanie announced. 'He won't give me his name. Shall I tell him you're busy?'

'What's he sound like?'

'He doesn't sound as barmy as some of them. He's quite well-spoken. Not particularly old. He's obviously got something on his mind.'

'OK, Stephanie, put him through.'

The connection was made and an anxious voice said, 'Is that Miss Epton?'

'Speaking.'

'May I come and see you, Miss Epton? I'm in urgent need of help.'

'What's your name?'

'What? Oh, I'm sorry . . . it's Nigel Ambrose.'

Chapter 10

Anyone of the name Ambrose had to be related to the late judge, Rosa reflected as she waited for him to arrive. But who exactly was Nigel Ambrose and what did he want? He had declined to say on the phone, telling her that he was in a call box and could be in her office within twenty minutes if she consented to see him.

'Please let me come!' he had urged her, and because she had had a boring day and was intrigued by the unexpectedness of his call she had agreed.

'Mr Ambrose has arrived,' Stephanie announced on the internal phone. Her tone was cool and detached which meant that their visitor had managed to arouse her hostility.

Rosa got up from her desk and went to the door to greet him. He gave her a limp handshake and what was obviously intended to be a winning smile, but which had the opposite effect. (Stephanie seldom erred in her judgement of the firm's clients.) Rosa reckoned he was in his early forties. He had brown hair, thinning on top and raggedly long at the back and his smile had revealed a row of stained teeth that could have kept a dentist busy for a week.

'You don't mind if I smoke, do you?' he said, as he sat down in her visitor's chair. He pulled out a packet of cigarettes and put one between his lips before Rosa could reply. 'I'm afraid I'm all on edge,' he went on, expelling a lungful of smoke. 'Would you like me to begin?'

Rosa gave a nod and reached for paper and pen. It was too late now, but she was beginning to regret having agreed to

51

see him. There was something shifty about him, as if he had spent too much time dodging out of sight round life's corners.

'Sir Edmund Ambrose was my uncle and I'm his ne'er-do-well nephew,' he said with a grimace of a smile. 'I saw you at the new court's opening two days ago, Miss Epton, but I don't expect you remember seeing me.'

'I'm afraid I don't.'

'I wasn't an official guest,' he went on with another attempt at an ingratiating smile. He paused and inhaled deeply before continuing. 'I suppose you know that the police have asked everyone who took photographs out on the balcony to come forward.'

'Yes.'

'I was one of them.'

'Well?'

'I don't know what I ought to do.'

Rosa put down her pen and fixed him with a steady look. 'You'd better start by telling me why you were at the ceremony. If you weren't invited and weren't on friendly terms with your uncle, what took you there?'

He nodded in a resigned way, as if he had feared this moment would arrive.

'I was last in touch with my uncle just after he divorced Heather. As you may know, she's now married to Judge Welford. Anyway, my uncle made it abundantly clear that the divorce hadn't changed anything where I was concerned. In other words, I was still a non-person in his life. OK, I know I've made a mess of my own life, but he's never lifted a finger to help me. He wasn't even prepared to give me money to stay away. He did give me the odd hundred pounds when I was starting out in adult life,' he went on grudgingly, 'but when I failed to settle down in a regular job he washed his hands of me. Didn't want to know I existed. Sometimes I'd feel so resentful and frustrated I'd try and phone him or I'd write him a letter, but it never got me anywhere. He'd put down the receiver as soon as he recognised my voice and he

52

never answered any of my letters.' He paused and added in a bitter tone, 'And one thing for absolute sure, I'm not mentioned in his will. He's probably left all his money to some law library. People meant nothing to him.'

'So why did you attend the opening ceremony?' Rosa asked, breaking the silence that had fallen.

'I was asked to go and take some photographs.'

'Who by?'

'You're not going to believe this, Miss Epton, but it's true. By a man in a pub.' He gave her a hopeful look. 'I used to live in Kilburn and still visit a pub in the area called the Queen's Head. A few weeks ago I got into conversation there with a coloured man who told me his name was Mervyn. He was friendly and better spoken than most of the regulars, and he was always rather flashily dressed. I told him my name was Nigel and mentioned, at some point, that I had an uncle who was a judge. He seemed to find this very funny and asked me my uncle's name. I used to see Mervyn at the Queen's Head two or three times a week and he always used to buy me a drink and enquire in a jokey way about my uncle. And then about ten days ago he asked me if I'd like to earn myself a hundred pounds. Well, Miss Epton, when your finances are in the state mine are, there's only one answer to that. Mind you, I was a bit wary as I didn't want to land myself in trouble and so I asked him what I had to do. "Just take a few photographs," he said casually. I told him I didn't have a camera and he laughed and said that would be taken care of. I'd be lent one. He then went on to say that a friend of his, whom he had told all about me, had once had the misfortune to be sent to prison by my uncle and had been waiting for the opportunity to get his own back in a harmless sort of way. Give the old bastard a nasty shock and leave him worried. This was so much my own sentiment that I probably agreed too readily,' he said ruefully. 'And remember we were enjoying a drink in a pub at the time. Anyway, Mervyn said the idea was for me to attend the opening of Runnymede Court, armed with a camera which his friend would supply. I had to make sure my uncle saw me, but, of course, I wasn't to speak to him. We agreed this would shake him . . .'

'How did Mervyn know your uncle would be at Runnymede Crown Court?' Rosa enquired.

'His friend had read it in the paper.'

'What was the name of Mervyn's friend?'

'He was always referred to as Fred.'

'Yes, go on,' Rosa said in a sceptical tone.

'Well, on the evening before the court opening, I met Mervyn at the Queen's Head and he handed me this camera. I didn't know the front of a camera from the back, but he showed me which button to press and said I didn't have to wind the film on afterwards as this happened automatically. The important thing was to ensure that my uncle saw me.'

'How did Mervyn know there'd be a session for photographs?'

'He didn't. He said I was to use the camera when I had an opportunity. He said there was bound to be a procession and all that mattered was that my uncle saw me taking photographs of him. It was reckoned this would give him the shock of his life. That evening I was to meet Mervyn in the pub and return the camera and tell him how it had gone. He had given me fifty pounds in advance and was going to give me the other fifty afterwards.'

'And did that part work out?'

'I went to the pub that evening, but Mervyn didn't turn up. A friend of his came and gave me the money and I handed him back the camera. He just came in and left again immediately. He wouldn't stop for a drink. He said Mervyn had sent him.'

'How many photographs did you take?'

'Only one. I just managed that before he fell into the river.'

'Were you pointing the camera directly at him?'

'I suppose so. I mean, I was trying to take one of him, but, for all I know, it could have been the sky.'

'But did you see him in the view-finder?'

He licked his lips. 'More or less, I think.'

54

'Did it look like an ordinary camera?'

'Yes, absolutely.'

'What make?'

'I've no idea.'

'Were you ever told what use was going to be made of the photograph?'

'No. The idea was just to give him a fright. There mayn't even have been a film in the camera for all I know.'

'And did your uncle recognise you?' Rosa asked.

A not particularly pleasant smile spread slowly across Nigel Ambrose's face. He nodded. 'He saw me all right. It was worth the price of admission just to see his expression.'

Rosa stared down at the few notes she had made. Without glancing up, she said, 'Did this whole business never strike you as being totally implausible? The idea of you and a camera just to give your uncle a fright on behalf of someone he'd once sent to prison?'

'Put like that it does sound a bit unlikely, I suppose. But when Mervyn and I talked about it in the Queen's Head it seemed no more than a practical joke.'

'For which you were to be paid a hundred pounds,' Rosa observed.

'I needed the money and I . . .' He gave her a mock smile. '. . . Well, I sympathised with the cause. My uncle was a bastard and I don't mind who knows it.'

That was one thing on which everyone seemed to be agreed, Rosa reflected.

'So what do you want me to do?' she asked in a none too enthusiastic voice.

'Tell me what to do! Ought I to go to the police or not?'

'Is there any reason to believe they can trace you?'

'Yes. One of the waiters recognised me as I was leaving. If the police question all the catering staff, he's bound to say he saw me there.' In a tone of disgust, he added, 'It was typical of my luck to bump into him.'

'I suppose you know the theory is that your uncle was hit by a poison pellet fired from a camera.'

'I've read that in the paper. That's why I'm here.'

Rosa became thoughtful. It was obvious that if he told the police what he had just told her, he would be an immediate suspect. He was probably one already. For not only would he have had opportunity, but it wouldn't be difficult to pin a motive on him as well. The story he had told her was preposterous. Nevertheless, experience had taught her that sometimes the most implausible stories were true. One thing stuck out, namely that if he didn't come forward, it would look that much worse when the police did catch up with him.

'Come and see me again tomorrow evening,' Rosa said at length. 'I'll be at the court tomorrow and I'll keep my ear to the ground. I'll be in a better position to advise you then.'

He gave a deep sigh. 'You've made me feel better already,' he said with a lopsided smile. 'I wasn't sure you'd believe my story.'

'I don't know that I do. It's one of the most implausible I've ever heard.'

'But it's true.'

'Either you're a knave or a fool, Mr Ambrose,' she remarked with a faint smile.

Rather to her surprise he laughed. 'I'm both. Sometimes more one. Sometimes more the other.'

'And in this instance?'

'Obviously more fool. Who but a fool could have landed himself in such a mess?'

It seemed to Rosa that the reply sprang a bit too readily to his lips.

Chapter 11

Detective Chief Superintendent Everson leaned forward with a concentrated expression like somebody engaged deeply in a game of chess. On the cleared surface of the desk in front of him about thirty photographs of varying sizes were set out. A few were in black and white, but most were in colour. From time to time he picked one up and examined it more closely, occasionally using a magnifying glass.

'This is the one that interests me,' he said to Inspector Martin as he reached for a large, blown-up one in black and white. 'It was taken by that freelance chap, Gary Lewis, only seconds before his lordship took his final dip. Look at the expression on his face! You can see that something's startled him.'

'His features seem to be registering a mixture of surprise and displeasure,' Martin remarked.

'It's the look of surprise that interests me. Displeasure was part of his normal expression. And it's more than surprise. He looks really startled. What do you think he suddenly saw?'

'Somebody he wasn't expecting to.' D.I. Martin was adept at supplying feedlines.

'Such as his nephew,' Everson said with a purr of satisfaction. 'Who else?'

'I agree, sir. We've got to find him.'

'But why hasn't he come forward? He must know about our appeal to all the photographers. And what was he doing there anyway? He obviously hadn't been invited. And if that waiter hadn't happened to recognise him, we'd never have known a damned thing about his being there.' He leaned back and laced his hands behind his head. 'I believe we could be on to something, David; thanks in this instance to a bit of luck.'

'Luck's as important in a murder enquiry as it is in backing winners,' Inspector Martin said with a grin.

'I don't back winners; or losers for that matter. Are you a betting man?' he asked suspiciously.

'I have been known to.' Martin quickly picked up another photograph. He had no wish to be quizzed by a Chief Superintendent about his considerable interest in horse racing. 'Have you noticed Judge Holtby's expression in this one, sir?' he said, thrusting it into Everson's hand. 'He, too, seems to have suffered a sudden shock. His eyes are a complete give-away.'

Everson turned the photograph over and read the name on the back. 'Which was Caroline Turner?'

'She's the daughter of the taxing officer.'

The photograph in question showed Judges Holtby and Welford in the middle of the picture with a partial view of Mr Justice Ambrose on one side and a beaming face poking itself determinedly into the picture on the other.

'I suppose that's her father,' Everson remarked drily.

'Yes. She took one of him on his own, but wanted to have one of him rubbing shoulders with the judiciary.'

Everson let out a derisive snort. 'Probably be sent out as the family Christmas card. But I agree about Judge Holtby's expression. We'd better ask him about it.'

With a thoughtful air he picked up one of the pictures taken by Adrian Burt, the photographer from the *Gazette*, and stared at it. It showed Mr Justice Ambrose in the act of toppling backwards. His arms were flung up and his scarlet robe had flown open to reveal a pin-striped leg and it was clear he had already lost his footing.

'That's the one for my personal album,' Everson remarked with a quick grin. He glanced at his watch. 'Find out if Judge Holtby is still on the premises and if we can have a word with him.'

Inspector Martin left the room and returned five minutes later.

'He's in his room, sir, and we can go along now.'

'Did you speak to him yourself?'

'No. Mr Dodd did. His court adjourned about forty-five minutes ago, but he's not yet left the building.'

'Good! Then let's go. Bring that photograph with you.'

Judge Anthony Holtby said the plaque on the door. It was a slat of wood with his name in shiny black letters and it fitted into a slot for easy removal, which seemed to emphasise the transitory nature of judges at Runnymede Crown Court.

It was a corner room with windows overlooking the river and the now flooded meadowland that bounded it. It was not a particularly large room, but it was comfortably furnished, one entire wall being taken up with bookshelves which were filled with newly bound copies of law reports and other legal volumes.

The judge was sitting at his desk with his back to one of the windows when the two officers were shown in by the usher who minded the judges' corridor. He rose as they entered and came round the desk to shake hands.

'Haven't seen you for a long time, Mr Everson,' he said. 'Not since the Bishop trial at the Old Bailey. Doubtless you remember the case? Two jury disagreements and then my client was convicted and got eight years at the third bite of the cherry. I always thought the prosecution was oppressive to go on after two juries had disagreed, but that'll hardly be your view. Anyway, you've not come here to reminisce. What is it you particularly want to talk about?'

'First of all, sir, my condolences at what's happened. I realise what a strain you and everyone else at the court must be working under.'

'Yes, it would be idle to pretend otherwise. Of necessity Judge Welford, Mr Dodd and myself are bearing the brunt. It's my further misfortune to be engaged on one of those

59

heavy drugs cases, which requires all my concentration and more.'

'Is that the case Mr Justice Ambrose was to have tried?' Everson asked.

'Yes. It had been fixed some time ago and with so many counsel involved it just had to go ahead as arranged.'

'I gather it was originally in your list, sir, but that Mr Justice Ambrose insisted on trying it himself. Is that correct?'

'It was his right, of course, as the visiting High Court judge to try any case he wanted.' Judge Holtby's tone was sharply defensive. 'Don't get the idea that we were like two dogs scrapping over a bone. When I told Mr Dodd I would take the case, I did so because I didn't think Mr Justice Ambrose would wish to become involved in a case of that probable length.'

'How long is it going to last?'

'Can't say. Could be up to three weeks. Might collapse a good deal earlier.'

'Collapse?'

Judge Holtby shifted in his chair. 'I shouldn't be discussing it as it has nothing whatsoever to do with your enquiries. What I've said you must regard as being off the record.'

'Naturally, sir. I certainly wasn't trying to lure you into indiscretion.'

'I'm sure you weren't, but let's move on to your next question.'

'When was the first moment you realised that something had happened to Mr Justice Ambrose?'

Judge Holtby closed his eyes for a moment. He looked suddenly grey with fatigue, as Everson gazed at him dispassionately. Nobody knew better than a senior C.I.D. officer what it was to work under stress, but equally senior C.I.D. officers couldn't afford to be sentimental. In any event, why should the demise of an unpopular judge be an occasion for any display of bereavement by a colleague who

60

presumably shared the general view? Furthermore, Judge Holtby was one of the few people against whom no sort of motive had been levelled. Plus the fact he couldn't possibly have committed the crime.

He opened his eyes and met Everson's gaze.

'I heard him let out a gasp and the next thing was he had fallen backwards over the balustrade. It was over in a matter of seconds. He was carried away downstream before our horrified eyes. As you probably know, he couldn't swim and I suppose the shock of immersion in icy water rendered him unconscious. At all events, he didn't appear to make any effort to try and save himself.'

'A pellet was found in his neck,' Everson said, 'and that may have had an immediate paralysing effect.'

Judge Holtby shivered. 'Is it true that it was poisoned?'

Everson nodded. 'Probably ricin, but I've not yet had the analyst's report. If it was ricin, it would have required prompt action to have saved his life or he'd have been dead within a day or so.'

'Who on earth could have wanted to kill him?' Before Everson could speak, Judge Holtby went on, 'Oh, I know he wasn't well liked, but if that was a criterion for murder, Scotland Yard would be worked even harder than it is. And who on earth could have thought up such a dramatic scenario?'

'It's certainly a puzzle,' Everson observed. 'Tell me, sir, did you have a good look at the people taking photographs out on the balcony?'

'I recognised one or two. There was Mrs Dodd and her son and a fellow from the *Gazette* and Judge Welford's brother. I can't recall seeing anyone else I knew.' After a slight pause he went on, 'There was quite a crowd and flashlights were popping all over the place. I chiefly remember wishing it would soon be over. I was conscious of Mr Justice Ambrose's distaste for the whole business, which makes it doubly terrible that it was the occasion of his death.'

'I understand your wife didn't attend the ceremony, sir?'

'She stayed away out of consideration for Mrs Welford, who, as you doubtless know, used to be Lady Ambrose.'

'Do you know anything about a nephew of Mr Justice Ambrose?'

'No. I know nothing of his family circumstances, other than what I've mentioned.'

Everson motioned Inspector Martin to hand him the photographs.

'Just have a look at this one, sir. Did you yourself see anything that might have caused the startled look on Mr Justice Ambrose's face?'

Judge Holtby took the photograph and studied it with an intense frown.

'No, I didn't,' he said slowly. 'Mr Justice Ambrose was always very much on his dignity and it's more than likely that one of the photographers was guilty of what he might consider to be *lèse majesté*. That would be quite sufficient to provoke the expression you see in this photograph.'

'Inspector Martin and I felt he had received a sudden shock.'

'If so, I've no idea what it could have been.'

Everson leaned forward and held out another photograph. 'Have a look at this one, sir,' he said, closely watching the judge's face. 'Can you recall what caused your look of surprise?'

It seemed that Judge Holtby's features became suddenly frozen. After a while he blinked as if testing the movements of his eyelids and then licked his lips. A little later he gave the two officers a small sickly smile.

'Dear oh dear, what a shattering art form photography can be! What on earth can I have been thinking when this one was taken?'

'What indeed, sir?'

'Frankly, I haven't the slightest idea what caused me to look like that.' He let out a nervous laugh. 'Almost like the rabbit that's caught sudden sight of the ferret.'

'But you don't recall seeing any ferrets there?'

'Leo Dodd's son bore the closest resemblance to a ferret, but for heaven's sake don't tell anyone I said that!' He laughed again, but in a forced way.

'Is there any significance in the gap between you and Mr Justice Ambrose?'

'None as far as I'm concerned.'

'You didn't deliberately leave a space between you?'

'Certainly not. I had no earthly reason to do so.' His tone was faintly belligerent.

'I only asked a simple question, sir.'

'Well, it has a simple answer. No, I did not deliberately leave a gap between myself and Mr Justice Ambrose.'

'One of the questions I've had to ask myself,' Everson said, 'is whether Mr Justice Ambrose was really the intended target.'

It seemed to Inspector Martin who was watching him intently that Judge Holtby's startled expression reflected that in the photograph he had just been shown.

'Good heavens! Who then? . . . I mean . . . surely you're not suggesting . . .'

'I'm not suggesting anything, sir. I was merely stating what had gone through my mind. After all, I gather there was a good deal of jostling amongst the photographers and it's occurred to me that in the confusion the murderer may have pointed his camera at the wrong person. But until we can establish a motive, it's no more than speculation. I take it that it's not occurred to you that you, for example, might have been the intended victim?'

'It certainly has not,' he said in a shaken voice.

'I know judges receive abusive and threatening letters from time to time, but you've not had any recently?'

'Neither recently, nor since I've been a judge.'

'What about Judge Welford?'

'I can't speak for him. We'd not been working at the same court until we joined forces here, though I've known him most of my professional life.' He glanced distractedly about the room. 'I believe he's already left the building and gone home.'

Everson made a non-committal sound and got up. 'I'll have a word with him tomorrow.'

'You mentioned motive just now,' Judge Holtby said in a tentative tone. 'Are you having difficulty establishing one?'

Everson looked at him keenly. Then with a slightly tigerish smile he said, 'The difficulty is in selecting the right one. So many people seem to have fallen foul of Mr Justice Ambrose, it's a question of finding the person who most wanted him out of the way. Have you any ideas on that, sir?'

'I'm afraid not,' Judge Holtby said quickly. 'I can't think why anyone should have chosen that particular moment to kill him.'

'That's the crux of the matter,' Everson observed. 'Why then?'

For some while after the two officers had left him, Judge Holtby stared out of the window as if mesmerised by the ceaseless flow of the river. He felt as if he had aged ten years in the past three days. His whole life had assumed an air of unreality and he yearned to wake up and find that he had been having a bad dream. Only habit and a robust constitution enabled him to carry on with anything approaching normality. Even so he knew it was obvious to everyone in court that he had failed to take a grip on the case he was trying. A judge needed to show his authority and never more so than when he had a number of strong counsel appearing in front of him. He had never cared for Henry Keffingham, nor did he trust him. He was equally aware that Keffingham had scant respect for his judicial competence.

For ten minutes or more he continued to gaze out of the window while his thoughts raced in unison with the rushing water. Then he swivelled his chair round and picked up the telephone.

'Hello, darling, it's me,' he said when he heard his wife's voice on the line. 'I shall be late home, so give yourself a drink and start the meal without me.'

'What's happened, Tony?' Denise asked with a note of

urgency.

'Nothing. It's just that I've got various things to attend to and it's easier to do them in the quiet of this building. You know what it's been like the last few days.'

'You sound so tired, Tony, why don't you come back and have a rest?'

'No, I'm all right. Tired, yes, but no more than to be expected.'

'How is your case going?' she asked anxiously.

'Let's not talk about that!' he said wearily. Then because his tone had been sharper than he intended, he added quickly, 'What sort of day have you had, darling?'

'I had a long talk with Heather Welford this morning. She called me. She's very worried for Stephen. She's frightened what the newspapers may say. Have you spoken to Stephen today?'

'No. He ate sandwiches in his room at lunchtime and rose early this afternoon, so I've not seen him other than disappearing along the corridor. Perhaps I'll call him when I get home this evening.'

'What time will that be?'

'I'm not certain, but don't worry! What's Ian been up to today?'

'He stayed in bed the whole morning and went off to meet a friend this afternoon. He didn't say when he'd be back. I'm worried about him, Tony.'

So what else is new, he felt like asking. Instead he said, 'I know you are, darling. It seems to me we spend our time as a family worrying about each other.' He tried to sound light-hearted, but knew he had failed.

With a promise that he would be home as soon as possible he rang off.

Five minutes later he got into his car and drove away.

It took him twenty minutes to reach the Greengage Club, which was his oasis when outside pressures threatened to become insupportable. It was small, select and so discreet as to be almost invisible. If you wanted to drink in unsocial

65

isolation, you could do so without risk of being accosted either by staff or by fellow members. Not that there ever seemed to be more than two or three people on the premises at any one time. And that included staff.

He knew that he shouldn't drink when he had to drive, but in his present frame of mind it seemed an unimportant risk, even for a judge.

Chapter 12

Although Everson still had the use of a room at the court, he had established his operational headquarters at a police station about two miles away and it was there that he held a conference the next morning.

'Whoever fired that pellet is guilty of murder even though it wasn't the direct cause of his lordship's death,' he declared to his assembled officers. 'That's point one. Point two is that it was obviously discharged from a weapon that resembled a camera. That means the murderer was in the line-up of photographers. All save two of whom have come forward and surrendered their cameras and film. The two who have not are Nigel Ambrose, his lordship's nephew, who was a gate-crasher at the ceremony, and a dark-haired youth who was next to Mrs Pitt and who seems to have melted away . . .'

'It's just possible, he never existed,' Inspector Martin interjected. 'I wouldn't regard Mrs Pitt as the most reliable of witnesses and her recollection was not at all clear.'

'As far as I'm concerned he exists and I want him traced,' Everson said firmly. 'If he doesn't exist, I want positive evidence of his non-existence,' he added equally firmly while Inspector Martin endeavoured to keep his eyebrows from shooting up. 'The other person who interests me is Barney Welford, brother of His Honour Judge Welford. There's something fishy about him. One witness thinks he had two cameras which could mean one for taking photographs and one for firing poison pellets. The pictures he took are lousy so he's obviously no photographer. It could be he was a better

67

marksman.'

'He's denied having a second camera,' Martin put in for the benefit of those who were receiving a first briefing. 'He says his deaf-aid must have been mistaken for a camera.'

'Do I take it, sir, that there's nothing suspicious about any of the other photographers?' The question came from Detective Sergeant Luke, recently back from a crime detection course and keen to impress his superior.

'You'd hardly expect there to be, would you?' Everson said a trifle militantly. 'If one of them was in possession of a fake camera, he'd hardly bring it along and hand it over to us. In fact, we'll be lucky if we find the weapon, but we've got to try and discover where it came from. It must have been manufactured somewhere.'

'Almost certainly abroad,' Martin said. In a knowledge-able tone he added, 'It's the sort of weapon used by Eastern European intelligence services.'

'Then we should ask our own intelligence people about it,' Everson said. 'They ought to be able to help.'

'Possession of such a sophisticated weapon opens up all sorts of interesting questions,' Sergeant Luke said with a serious frown. 'It implies a background of money and careful planning.'

'So what's one of these interesting questions?' Everson asked with a touch of impatience.

'Who, for example, had access to such a wide range of resources?' Sergeant Luke said, looking round the assembled faces with a pleased smirk.

'Not only who, but why was that particular moment chosen?' Martin added. 'That's what we should be asking ourselves.'

'I have been asking myself,' Everson remarked testily. 'But we're not going to find the answers sitting round the table.'

The next twenty minutes or so were taken up in an allocation of duties. To Sergeant Luke's disgust, he was told to trace the missing photographer and establish whether or not he existed. It was a task that would involve a lot of slogging routine and he found it hard to hide his chagrin. He had hoped to be put in charge of liaising with Interpol and the intelligence services regarding the provenance of the weapon.

But as Everson remarked to Martin afterwards, 'They invariably need taking down a peg or two when they've been on those courses and had their heads stuffed with a lot of high-falutin' ideas.'

Inspector Martin suspected that the observation had been addressed as much *at* him as to him. However, he had considerable respect for his Detective Chief Superintendent, who though he might belong to the old school of police officer was nobody's fool.

At about the time that Everson's meeting ended, Barney Welford called his brother.

'I would have rung you last night, but my damned phone was out of order,' he said when he got through. 'Thought it better to call you at home before you left for court. Never know who may be listening in at that place. I've handed in my camera and film like a good boy,' he went on. 'Doubt whether my pictures were much help to anybody. I gather I may expect a visit from the police fairly soon and I thought I should let you know, Stephen. Not that I can tell them much, of course. How's Heather bearing up?'

'She's all right. The police spent quite a time questioning her yesterday. They wanted to know the background to her divorce. She seems to have dealt with them very competently, but it's not much fun for either of us. It's like wondering whether a storm is about to break overhead,' he added bleakly.

'And all on account of that old bastard! I know one shouldn't speak ill of the dead, but as I was given to speaking ill of him when he was alive, I don't see why I should stop now. He was an old bastard!' He paused and then went on in a lowered tone, 'Any theories as to who did it? I imagine the police have taken you and Tony Holtby into their confidence.'

His brother let out a derisive laugh. 'We're more likely to be on their short list of suspects.'

'But that's crazy, Stephen. Neither of you could possibly have killed him.'

'No, but either of us could have instigated the crime. With their tortuous minds, they could decide that I had a motive: that Ambrose had some hold over me as a result of what happened in the past.' There was a silence and Judge Welford said, 'Are you still there, Barney?'

'Yes, I was thinking.'

'What?'

'If it hadn't been for me you'd never have met Heather.'

'Why do you suddenly say that?' his brother asked suspiciously.

'And if you'd never met Heather, none of this would ever have happened.'

'For heaven's sake, Barney! If you carry the chain of causation to those lengths you'll become a morbid wreck.'

'Don't rub it in!'

'I'm sorry. You know I didn't mean *that*. I wasn't referring to your illness. Nobody's faced life with more courage than you have since your stroke.' Stephen Welford's heart sank as he realised his brother had begun to cry. One of the effects of his stroke had been to make him weepy. 'Look, why not come to supper this evening and we can have a long talk about everything?'

'I'm all right. I just don't want to be a burden to you. All I want you to know, Stephen, is that I'm so proud of you and would do anything in the world to help you.'

'I know you would, Barney, and I'm ever grateful. Don't worry about Heather and me, we'll weather this storm all right.' In a lighter tone he went on, 'How are you getting on with your new hearing aid? I noticed on that awful day you'd gone back to your old contraption.'

'I'm slowly getting used to the new one.'

70

'Well, persevere with it. It'll be much lighter and more convenient.'

'Yes,' he said in a curiously abstracted voice.

'Well, I must drive to court. Phone Heather later and let her know about supper this evening. In any event we'll keep in close touch.'

Chapter 13

Rosa was still undecided, as she drove to court that morning, how much of Nigel Ambrose's story she believed. Of one thing she was more than certain, however, Chief Superintendent Everson would accept only those parts that suited him and would reject the rest. He would be willing to see Mr Justice Ambrose's nephew as a murderer, but hardly as the innocent fool he made himself out to be. And who would blame him? At all events Rosa had made up her mind to approach Everson and give him the gist of her client's story and arrange an interview at which she would insist on being present.

She had considered the alternative, which was to advise Nigel Ambrose to lie low and leave the police to find him if they could. The trouble was that they undoubtedly would and then his situation would be infinitely worse. Moreover, she had in mind that, if he had been manipulated as he asserted, it was possible that those who had so used him would pull the mat from under his feet at their own convenience.

It seemed more than likely that the camera he was given by Mervyn in the Queen's Head was the murder weapon. She suspected that, despite his protestations to the contrary, he must now be well aware of it himself. Must, in fact, have been so since he pressed the button to take a photograph and discharged a poison pellet instead. It was, indeed, a grim predicament in which he found himself. Fortunately the ethics of her profession didn't require her to believe in his innocence, she only had to advance his account of events as persuasively as possible. But what a task that was! And, anyway, why had Mervyn and those further in the background wanted to despatch Mr Justice Ambrose in such an elaborate manner? These were questions the police would have to follow up however sceptical they were about his story.

As her thoughts swung to and fro, her mind invariably returned to one question. Was Nigel Ambrose a fool or a knave? If the former, her advice was probably correct; if the latter, it was almost certainly not. On balance she was inclined to believe his role on this occasion had been that of fool. In which case the sooner she had a word with Everson the better.

Nevertheless, it was in a mood of little confidence that she drove into the car park of Runnymede Crown Court that morning.

She was still sitting in her car lost in thought when a figure loomed at the driver's window.

'Good morning, Miss Epton,' Bernard Blaker said with his usual grave courtesy. 'I saw you park and you failed to get out, so I thought I'd come and see if you were all right.'

'Yes, I'm perfectly all right, thank you. I was just deep in thought,' she said, conjuring up a smile.

He opened the door and held it for her to get out. His vicuna coat was draped casually over his shoulders and he gave the impression of having come straight from an expensive men's shop wrapped in cellophane.

'Any further developments in the murder case?' he enquired in a conversational tone.

'Not that I'm aware of,' she said somewhat defensively.

'I only wondered. To be honest, I'm rather more interested in my own case. Mr Justice Ambrose's death is only a distraction as far as I'm concerned. It seems that nobody here can think of anything else, but I suppose that's only natural. I merely hope it doesn't have an adverse effect on our trial.'

Rosa frowned. 'I don't see how it can.'

'Well, it's obviously had an effect on Judge Holtby, wouldn't you say? And on the clerk of the court, too.'

'I'm sure it's having no effect whatsoever on your trial,' Rosa replied with a good deal more confidence than she felt. What she of course meant was that it was not having any disadvantageous effect from the defendants' point of view. If Judge Holtby was affected by what had happened it could only benefit Blaker and his co-defendants, for in the event of a confused summing-up the jury would take the line of least resistance and acquit. How justice might eventually be served was a different matter! She was not, however, disposed to canvass that particular nicety with her client.

Inside the court-house she excused herself and went in search of Everson only to be told that he hadn't arrived and that it was not known when, if at all, he would be turning up that day. The Detective Constable to whom she spoke offered to relay a message, but Rosa told him not to bother.

'You look harassed and out of breath, Rosa,' Paul Elson said when they bumped into one another at the court entrance.

'I'm both. I thought I was going to be late.'

'And what makes you harassed?' Elson said with an enquiring grin.

'The thought of being late,' Rosa replied with a smile as forthcoming as a steel door.

Elson chuckled. In his view, Rosa Epton was as tough as they came and yet could also be sweeter than honey. Despite her elfin appearance and her obvious femininity she was able to stand up to anyone in the rough and tumble of criminal practice. Elson, whom she frequently briefed, held her in high professional respect and was also very fond of her as a person. She had visited his home more than once and not only got on famously with his wife, but was on equally popular terms with his children. No mean feat, he reckoned.

Together they made their way into court and a few minutes later Judge Holtby took his seat.

If anything he looked more ill than he had the previous

day. As Paul Elson whispered to Jane Crenlow, the bags beneath his eyes hung like small gourds.

When the court had adjourned the previous afternoon a senior customs officer had been in the witness box and was about to produce written statements made by Henry Keffingham's client and two other defendants. These contained damaging admissions and Keffingham had indicated that he wished to contest their admissibility.

'You won't get anywhere with that line,' Nicholas Barrow said confidently to his opponent. 'Those statements were taken impeccably. I assure you the officer didn't put a foot wrong.'

'We'll see,' was all that Keffingham had replied.

'I believe you wish to address the court in the absence of the jury, Mr Keffingham,' Judge Holtby said, as if bracing himself for a walk in lashing rain and a force ten gale.

'If your honour pleases.'

The judge turned towards the jury and explained that what was about to take place in their absence was a trial within a trial to enable him to rule on the admissibility of certain evidence. In due course they would be brought back to court and would learn his decision.

The senior customs officer, Howard Beeston by name, was a burly man who had given evidence in countless cases and who felt strongly that if anyone's word deserved to be believed in court it was that of himself and his colleagues in their unremitting efforts to prosecute drug smugglers to conviction. He now faced Henry Keffingham who stood ready to cross-examine him on behalf of Gail Bristow.

'Did you not tell the defendant that if she made a confession she might not be prosecuted?' Keffingham asked without preliminary word.

'Certainly not,' the witness replied in an outraged tone. 'It would have been most improper.'

'Exactly. But it's what you said to her, isn't it?'

'No, never,'

'Didn't you tell her you were after bigger fish and that she

75

could help herself by making a confession?'

'I certainly did not.'

'Did you tell her that, if she refused to sign a confession, you would, to use your own expression, hot up the evidence against her?'

'That's an outrageous suggestion.'

'But it's true, isn't it?'

'No, it is not,' Beeston said angrily, looking towards the judge for protection.

But Judge Holtby studiously avoided the witness's tacit plea and remained bent over his notebook.

'Did you tell her she was far too attractive to be caught up in drug smuggling?'

The witness hesitated. 'I may have said I was surprised she had allowed herself to become involved,' he said in a schoolmasterish voice.

'Is it not a fact that you used both threats and cajolery in obtaining that statement?'

'Certainly not. I bent over backwards to be fair to the defendant.'

'To the extent that you refused to allow her to phone her solicitor?'

'I told her she could speak to him later.'

'After you had extracted a confession from her?'

'That's a wicked allegation.' The witness once more glanced indignantly towards the judge, but to no effect.

'She was very distressed throughout the interview, was she not?'

'I wouldn't say so.'

'Weeping and asking to be put in touch with her lawyer?'

'No.'

'Not weeping?'

'She may have shed a tear or two,' Beeston said with a sneer, 'but I'd describe them as crocodile tears rather than genuine ones.'

'But at least you recognised them as tears?'

The witness gave a dismissive shrug.

And so the cross-examination continued for another fifteen minutes until Keffingham reached his final question.

'Is it not a fact that in the last three cases in which you have given evidence for the prosecution, the defendants have all been acquitted?'

'That's a most improper question, your honour,' Barrow declared, bouncing to his feet.

Judge Holtby gazed morosely first at prosecuting counsel and then at Henry Keffingham.

'Even if the answer to the question is yes,' he said, 'it doesn't follow that the acquittals were due to the evidence of this witness.'

'Perhaps I might put a supplementary question, your honour,' Keffingham said. Without waiting for the judge's reply he turned to the witness and went on, 'In each case were written statements you had obtained from the defendants ruled as inadmissible by the trial judge?'

Beeston flushed angrily. 'I can explain that perfectly well,' he growled.

'Just answer yes or no,' defending counsel growled back.

'Yes, but . . .'

'Thank you, your honour, I have no further questions to ask this witness,' Keffingham said, and sat down with an air of triumph.

'I suggest, your honour,' Barrow spluttered, 'that in the interests of justice and fairness, the witness be allowed to finish what he was about to say.'

The judge shifted uncomfortably in his chair. 'I think better not. I shall ignore what has just been adduced when I come to decide this issue.'

Barrow proceeded to re-examine the witness with a view to restoring his damaged credibility, after which Keffingham called Gail Bristow into the witness box.

She was an attractive girl with an air of innocence, genuine or calculated according to which side anyone was on. She said she had only signed the statement after a lengthy period of mental torture, during which all her requests to see a

77

lawyer had been refused. She had been put under so much pressure and subjected to such bullying tactics that she didn't know what she was saying and had finally signed the statement when she was at breaking-point.

In cross-examination Barrow suggested her account was a gross distortion of the truth; that she had been caught red-handed, had been treated with total propriety and had never been put under any sort of pressure from start to finish. At this she gave prosecuting counsel a sad little smile and said, alas, it had been just as she described.

Since the counsel representing Yarfe and Watt realised this was a rolling bandwagon on to which they should also jump, it was agreed that Judge Holtby should reserve his decision until the end.

Beeston, who by now had assumed a thoroughly beleaguered air, nevertheless vigorously refuted each allegation, though with less and less confidence as the assault went on. Giving evidence under cross-examination is intellectually exhausting at the best of times, but when a witness is subjected to a barrage of hostile questioning his mental agility sooner or later starts to flag.

Eventually, however, his ordeal reached an end and all eyes fell on the judge as the court awaited his ruling. For a couple of minutes he sat heavily frowning, as if contemplating a choice of words. Then he said abruptly, 'The court will adjourn for ten minutes.'

'What's that in aid of?' Barrow said fretfully to Henry Keffingham as soon as the judge had departed.

'Probably wants to pee,' Keffingham replied.

'He must have made up his mind, so what's he want to adjourn for?' Barrow repeated. 'Tony Holtby's normally quick and decisive on issues like this.'

'He's not shown much decisiveness in this case up till now,' Jane Crenlow observed. 'What are you going to do, Nicholas, if he rules against the statements?'

'How can he do that?' prosecuting counsel said tetchily.

'You won't have much of a case left without the

78

statements,' Keffingham remarked with a complacent smile.

'One thing for sure, Ambrose would never have let you get away with that unscrupulous attack on the unfortunate Beeston.' It was apparent that Nicholas Barrow had been needled almost as much as the witness himself.

'Unscrupulous, indeed!' Keffingham retorted. 'It was a straightforward frontal assault on an arrogant witness. If you want to use that word, use it against the bully-boys from bureaucratic agencies who come into our courts and expect every word of their evidence to be accepted as unsullied gospel. It does them good to be knocked about a bit. Anyway, it's never more than a fraction of the treatment they invariably mete out to the unfortunates who fall into their clutches.'

Barrow had listened with an expression of increasing disdain. He now said in a lofty tone, 'I suppose it depends on whose side you are.'

'I'm on my client's side, of course.'

'I didn't mean that,' prosecuting counsel said with a sniff. 'I happen to think the police and customs and other law enforcement agencies do a splendid job and get very little thanks for it.'

'I don't subscribe to such sweeping generalisations,' Keffingham remarked. 'As far as I'm concerned, your witness was a smug, pontificating bully and I'd be on the side of anyone who came up against him in the course of his work. What's more he'd commit perjury as readily as he'd plant a packet of heroin in your hip pocket.'

Nicholas Barrow pulled his gown around him and turned an indignant shoulder on the perpetrator of so much subversive talk. Jane Crenlow, who had been listening with an air of detachment, now gave Rosa an amused smile.

'You still haven't answered Jane's question as to what course you'll take if Tony Holtby excludes the statements,' Keffingham went on, unabashed by his colleague's reaction.

But the only response was a heavy pursing of the lips, at which Jane gave Rosa a further smile. It seemed to say, aren't men children when they quarrel? As she had no particular regard for either of the counsel concerned it had been easy to remain neutral. Keffingham she didn't entirely trust as a professional colleague and Barrow was a plain bore.

Luckily before Keffingham could rekindle the argument, Judge Holtby returned to court.

He had barely sat down before he began speaking in a low, rapid tone. Without looking up from his notes, he said, 'In my view the prosecution has not discharged the onus of proving that these statements were made voluntarily and I accordingly rule against their admissibility.' He glanced towards prosecuting counsel. 'Do you wish to say anything, Mr Barrow, before the jury return to court?'

'I can't, of course, do other than accept your honour's decision,' Barrow said stiffly. 'Perhaps I might be allowed a few minutes to consult with those instructing me.'

'Very well, I'll adjourn for fifteen minutes,' the judge said with a relieved air and departed once more from the bench.

'It's an incredible decision,' Barrow muttered petulantly. 'He must be ill or something.'

Henry Keffingham grinned. 'Your trouble, Nicholas, is that you think all your geese are swans. You should do more defending and less prosecuting and then you'd be less prone to righteous indignation.' He turned to Jane Crenlow. 'Without the statements he hasn't a case against three of the defendants and the case against your client was always paper thin unless Watt gave evidence for the crown, and that's obviously not going to happen now.'

'I hope not.'

'You make sure it doesn't, my love. Anyway, Watt must know now which side his bread is buttered. Helping the prosecution has no mileage in it for him once he's been acquitted. It was only while they could dangle the prospect of a light sentence in front of him that he might have been tempted.'

Jane Crenlow, who could have done without this homily, moved along to where she could speak to David Pilly, who was Watt's counsel.

80

'If the prosecution throw in their hand against your client, David, I take it there'll be no question of his agreeing to give evidence against mine?'

'Once he's been acquitted, I doubt whether you'll see his heels for dust. He's a thoroughly frightened little man who felt he was poised between the devil and the deep blue sea.' He smiled. 'The devil, of course, being your client. Anyway, I'll go and have a word with my instructing solicitor and give him my view.'

About five minutes later, Barrow, who had been outside in consultation with his junior counsel and the solicitor representing the Customs and Excise Department, not to mention various customs and police officers, returned to court.

'In the light of the judge's inexplicable ruling,' he said to the assembled defending counsel, 'it's been decided that the prosecution will offer no further evidence.' Looking at Jane Crenlow he went on, 'I'm told that Watt would not be prepared to give evidence for the crown and although one can't say there is no evidence against your client . . .'

'I can and, at the proper moment, would,' Jane broke in.

'Be that as it may,' Barrow went on, frowning at the interruption, 'I have advised those instructing me that I see little merit in continuing a case against somebody who would, in present circumstances, be likely to get out on a submission of no case to answer at the conclusion of the prosecution's evidence.'

'I applaud your advice,' Jane murmured drily.

'And now I'd better find Leo Dodd and tell him what I'm proposing to do.'

The clerk had been popping in and out of court all morning wearing a perpetually preoccupied air.

Normally he would have been on hand to learn what course of action counsel had in mind and have been ready to go and inform the judge. But he had shot out of court as soon as Judge Holtby announced the adjournment and had not reappeared.

It was while Barrow was staring somewhat petulantly at the door through which the clerk made his entrances and exits that Dodd appeared.

'I was just coming to look for you,' prosecuting counsel said in a reproving tone. 'I've already told my learned friends the course I'm proposing to take.'

When Barrow had finished, Dodd gave a small nod, but made no comment.

'You'd better go and tell him before he comes back on the bench,' Barrow said when the clerk showed no sign of moving.

'I'll leave you to do that in open court,' Dodd replied.

Barrow stared at him in surprise. 'Won't he expect to be told before he returns?'

'He'll send for me if he does. Otherwise he can hear it first-hand from you.'

Barrow shrugged and turned away. It seemed to him that everything and everyone at Runnymede Crown Court had turned sour.

'His honour wants to know if you're ready yet?' an usher enquired of prosecuting counsel.

'Yes.'

A minute later Judge Holtby returned to the bench and Barrow informed him of the decision not to proceed further with the case.

The judge said nothing, but nodded gravely. Then he gave a further nod in the direction of the jury bailiff who was hovering near the door which led to the jury's retiring room.

As they filed back into court, only the four defendants seemed to pay them any attention. Counsel lounged back in their seats and stared at whatever took their fancy – ceiling or the back of the head in front of them.

Rosa tidied up her papers and then sat with her hands folded in her lap. She felt no sense of satisfaction at the outcome, even though it involved her client's acquittal.

Once the jury was seated, the judge addressed them.

'Members of the jury, I'm sorry you have been kept

waiting for so long, but I had to hear counsel's submissions as to the admissibility of certain written statements made by their clients. This involved hearing evidence as to the manner in which the statements were obtained. As a result I have ruled, as a matter of law, that these statements should not be admitted in evidence.' He turned and gave prosecuting counsel a questioning look.

'Yes, Mr Barrow, you have something to tell the court?'

Nicholas Barrow then informed his honour once more, this time at considerably greater length, what he had told him in the absence of the jury a few minutes earlier. When he sat down, Judge Holtby turned again to the jury.

'Members of the jury, these defendants are in your charge and you are accordingly required to return verdicts in respect of each of them. On my direction you should find them not guilty. Will the foreman kindly stand up and do as I have directed.'

Outside the court, Bernard Blaker shook hands with Jane Crenlow and Paul Elson and thanked them gravely for their services.

'In the event we didn't have much to do,' Jane observed.

'Perhaps not. But you might have had a fight on your hands.'

'It would certainly have been tougher going in front of Mr Justice Ambrose,' Paul Elson said.

'Then I must be thankful that he didn't try the case, if I may say so without offending you. I'm probably biassed, but I thought Judge Holtby handled the case very fairly.'

There was an awkward silence before Jane Crenlow said, 'Well, I must be getting back to London.'

'Me, too,' Elson said quickly.

'Thank you, too, Miss Epton,' Blaker said when the others had gone. 'I had complete confidence in you from the outset.' Rosa made a deprecating gesture and he went on, 'Oh, I know yours is a less glamorous role than counsel's, but it's a solicitor who has to supply the material from which counsel makes the bullets.'

'In this case, none had to be fired,' she remarked with a quick laugh.

'I'm sure we'll be in touch again before long,' he said as they shook hands.

Not if I can help it, Rosa thought as she watched him stroll confidently towards the main entrance. She had found their conversation uncomfortable and was glad to disengage herself from his company. In due course she would be sending him a bill, but that wouldn't necessitate a meeting.

She glanced at her watch. With luck Chief Superintendent Everson was somewhere in the building and she could have a quiet word with him.

The same detective constable to whom she had spoken in the morning informed her, however, that he hadn't been in all day and wasn't expected.

'He's dashed up to town,' he told Rosa. 'They've traced a suspect they were looking for.'

'Who?' Rosa asked anxiously.

'Probably shouldn't tell you, but it's the old judge's nephew.'

Chapter 14

Even as she asked the question Rosa knew what the answer was going to be. If only she had been able to speak to Everson that morning . . . Now she had lost an advantage. The fact that it was hardly her fault was small consolation. Instead of being able to take the initiative, it had been seized from her.

'Do you know where Mr Everson is?' she asked with a weary sigh.

'No, but I can probably find out.'

'I'd be grateful.' The young D.C. gave her a quizzical look so that she felt obliged to explain. 'The judge's nephew is my client.'

His look changed to one of surprise and then to one of suspicion.

'If you'd like to hang on, I'll find out what I can.' In a faintly embarrassed tone he added, 'Perhaps you wouldn't mind waiting outside while I make some enquiries.'

Rosa nodded. 'Of course. If you do get through to Mr Everson, tell him that Mr Ambrose has only been my client since last night. I wouldn't want him to think that I've been hiding him under wraps.'

'I'll tell him that.'

Rosa went out into the corridor and walked towards a window at the end which overlooked the swollen river. To the right she could see the weir from which Mr Justice Ambrose's body had been recovered like a piece of flotsam. She found it hard to believe it had happened only three days ago. So much seemed to have happened since then.

'Miss Epton?'

She turned to see the young D.C. with his head round the door. As she retraced her steps he disappeared inside the room and was on the phone when she got there. A moment later he replaced the receiver and looked at her a trifle nervously.

'I understand that the person you're interested in is being interviewed at Colne Police Station,' he said in an official voice.

'Is that the new station the other side of Staines?' He nodded. 'So he's been brought down here?'

'Yes.'

'Is Colne where Mr Everson has established his operational headquarters?'

'Yes.'

'I'd better go along there.'

'I'm not too sure you'll be allowed to see him.'

Rosa frowned. 'Is that what you've been told to tell me?'

'I was led to understand that the interview was at a delicate stage,' he said with an embarrassed squirm. 'It might be better . . .'

'Then I've no time to lose,' Rosa broke in firmly. 'Thanks for your help.'

He watched her depart with a sigh of relief. Let his superiors cope with this determined female! He had not found it an easy situation to handle. He liked to believe he could be tough when occasion demanded, but it invariably left him feeling emotionally drained so that he sometimes wondered if he had chosen the right career.

When Rosa arrived at Colne Police Station and announced her presence, she was politely asked to take a seat while an officer went to find out if Chief Superintendent Everson was available. The officer in question managed to convey the impression that he was setting off on a lengthy voyage of discovery and that quick results shouldn't be expected.

About ten minutes later Detective Inspector Martin appeared and introduced himself to Rosa.

86

'I'm sorry to have kept you waiting, Miss Epton,' he said blandly. 'I understand you're Mr Ambrose's solicitor.'

'Yes.'

'Well, as you've already been told, he's at this station and is helping us with our enquiries into his uncle's murder.'

'May I see him please?'

'Oh, certainly.'

'Now?'

Inspector Martin shook his head slowly as though genuinely saddened by having to reject her request.

'I'm afraid it's not convenient at this moment. He's helping us voluntarily and it'd be better if his concentration wasn't disturbed by an outside intrusion.'

Rosa gazed at him much as David probably fixed Goliath with a first appraising look.

'Am I to understand you're refusing me access to my client?' she said in a steely voice.

'Not refusing, Miss Epton . . .'

'What then?'

'You'll certainly be able to see him in due course.'

'I'm not interested in that, I demand to see him now.'

Inspector Martin sighed. 'The police have a duty towards the public in the investigation of crime and it would not be in the public interest for you to see him at this stage. We are within our rights, Miss Epton.'

'Are you proposing to charge him?' she asked bleakly.

'I'm not in a position to answer that question. By which I mean that no decision has yet been taken.'

'How long are you proposing to hold him incommunicado?'

'No longer than we have legal power to do so.'

'Does that mean he will be charged within the next twenty-four hours or be released?'

'I'm sure it'll be one or the other before then.'

'And in the meantime you're refusing to let me see my client?'

'As I've tried to explain, Miss Epton, seeing him

87

prematurely could prejudice our enquiries.'

Rosa realised there was no point in continuing to beat her head against the wall. It was a situation with which she was extremely familiar. The police had detained a suspect and were not going to let him see his lawyer until it suited them. She had sometimes found bluster and dire threats to succeed, but clearly not with the present investigating team. She and Martin both knew it was too soon for her to invoke the law. Provided the police could show they were not detaining her client unreasonably, they could ward off any legal action. The courts always accepted that there were occasions when suspects could be held and questioned without interference, especially when, as Martin had quickly told her, her client had gone to the station voluntarily. That probably meant no more than that he hadn't actually been dragged screaming through the streets. All the police needed to say at this stage was that her intervention could prejudice their enquiries and it was certainly too soon to start thinking about a writ of *habeas corpus*.

As Rosa and Inspector Martin stared across a table at one another, each was pretty well able to read the other's mind. It was a game in which the moves were as formalised as those in chess.

'I would like it on record that I was refused access to my client,' Rosa now said.

'The police wouldn't deny it,' Martin replied with a faint smile. 'If you'll leave me your telephone number, I'll contact you as soon as we've completed this stage of our enquiries.'

'I've already told Mr Ambrose not to make any written statements to the police,' Rosa said without complete truth. 'If he does make one, I'll know that it must have been obtained by improper means.'

Inspector Martin cocked his head on one side as if listening for something beyond the four walls of the room.

'I can't hear any screams or yells for mercy,' he remarked amiably.

Rosa felt depressed as she returned to her car. It was pure

bad luck that the police had got hold of Nigel Ambrose before she could do what she had intended. They had obviously made a vigorous and successful search for him while she had been shut away in Judge Holtby's court. Even if he was a client of only one day, events had left her feeling dispirited and frustrated.

It took her thirty minutes to drive back to London and she went immediately home. She phoned Stephanie in the office to tell her that the Blaker case had finished and that she would probably spend most of the next day at her desk. She would like to have talked to her partner, Robin Snaith, but it appeared he was interviewing a client at Ashford Remand Centre.

At eight o'clock that evening she left her flat dressed in a chunky maroon sweater, a pair of jeans and a quilted driving jacket, giving her the overall appearance of someone setting off on a trans-polar expedition. But there was a threat of further snow in the air and, like most thin people, she always felt the cold.

It took her a bare fifteen minutes to reach the street in Kilburn in which the Queen's Head public house was located.

The saloon bar had about a dozen people in it, most of them sitting round the edge of the room. There were not more than two or three propping up the bar itself. Of the two coloured men present neither came near to fitting her mental picture of flashily dressed Mervyn. She approached one end of the counter where a barmaid with spiky strawlike hair was closely examining her face in a cracked wall mirror. It was several seconds before she became aware of Rosa's presence.

'Sorry, luv, I didn't know you was waiting,' she said, giving a final peer at her face in the mirror. 'Something's 'appened to my skin. It's bloody awful.'

'I can't see anything wrong with it,' Rosa said comfortingly.

'Really? Well, if it doesn't look awful, it feels it. I think it's some make-up I was given for my birthday. Probably comes from China or one of those sort of places. Made of ground-up insects most likely. Anyway, what do you want, luv?'

Rosa asked for a glass of dry white wine. While the barmaid was fetching it, she glanced around and found that a number of lone drinkers had her under scrutiny, including one tall and graceful coloured youth who was lounging in a corner with a pint of beer in front of him. He was dressed entirely in black leather which gave him a somewhat sinister appearance. When he reached for his glass, Rosa noticed two heavy gold rings on his right hand.

'It's nice and cold,' the barmaid said, handing Rosa her glass of wine.

Rosa thanked her and pushed a pound note across the counter. When the barmaid brought her change, Rosa said, 'Do you happen to know if Mervyn's here this evening?'

'Not seen 'im for a week or more. Used to come in regular at one time. 'Appens with a lot of customers; they're 'ere every night and then they suddenly disappears.' She gazed round the room. 'Can only see two in 'ere this evening who've been coming for more than a few months. That old boy in the far corner and Magda near the door.' Rosa glanced to where a female with mauve hair, a mauve face and mauve clothes was delicately sipping at a gin and tonic. 'She may look like a fallen plum, but she's all right. You could fill a swimming-pool with the amount of gin she gets through in a year.' She turned her attention back to Rosa. 'You local?'

'I live in the Notting Hill area,' Rosa said. It always sounded more egalitarian than Kensington which still made people think of a more upper crust society.

'Thought I'd not seen you 'ere before,' the barmaid said, scowling at her complexion in the mirror.

'You don't know how I could get in touch with Mervyn, do you?' Rosa asked.

The girl assumed a thoughtful frown. 'Trying to think who I've seen 'im talking to.' After a slight pause she went on, 'There was a chap 'e used to drink with, but I 'aven't seen 'im for a few days.'

Rosa gave a thumbnail sketch of Nigel Ambrose and the barmaid said, 'Yes, that's the fellow. You know 'im?'

'Yes. I need to get in touch with Mervyn on his behalf.'

'No one in trouble, I 'ope?'

'No, nothing like that,' Rosa said quickly.

At that moment the coloured youth arrived at the bar and ordered another pint of beer. While it was being drawn, he stared unashamedly at Rosa who pretended to ignore his scrutiny.

'Did I hear you say you were looking for Mervyn?' he said in a husky tone. His speech was perfectly articulated, in keeping with his general appearance.

Rosa turned her head slowly in his direction. 'Yes. Are you a friend of his?'

'Bring your drink over to the table,' he said, leading the way. When they were seated he asked, 'Why do you want to see Mervyn?'

'I want to talk to him.'

'What about?'

'That's between me and Mervyn,' Rosa replied, matching stare for stare.

He shrugged an elegant shoulder. 'I might be able to help you if you told me why you wanted to see him.'

Rosa was thoughtful for a moment. This was the sort of game that need have no end until one of the participants fell off his chair from boredom.

'He loaned a camera to someone I know,' she remarked, deciding to break the impasse.

He nodded slowly, never taking his eyes off her face. They were particularly lustrous eyes and gave him an unfathomable expression. He had a perfect smooth skin and finely sculptured features. Rosa put his age at about nineteen or twenty and thought he probably had at least ten percent white blood in his veins.

'Couldn't have been Mervyn,' he said. 'He doesn't have a camera.'

'Nevertheless, he loaned one to my friend,' Rosa declared

firmly.

She was still waiting for his reply when he suddenly rose and made quickly for the exit. He had disappeared almost before she realised what had happened. At the same moment she became aware of two men talking to the barmaid who was nodding in Rosa's direction. They now came over to where she was sitting. Just as her companion had obviously identified them as police officers, so did Rosa.

'Excuse me, miss,' said the burly one with a gingery moustache, 'I understand you've been asking for Mervyn. We're police. I'm Detective Sergeant Holland and this is Detective Constable France.' He paused and added with a poker face, 'And we're not here on behalf of the Common Market. Sorry if I've spoilt your own little joke, but I always try and get it in first. May I ask what your interest is in Mervyn?'

'I want to talk to him about a camera.'

His eyes narrowed. 'Go on, miss.'

'I'm a solicitor and I represent somebody whom your colleagues are interviewing in connection with the death of Mr Justice Ambrose.'

The two officers exchanged a quick glance. 'And why do you come looking for him here?' Sergeant Holland enquired.

'Because this is where the story began as far as my client is concerned.'

'I gather you don't know this Mervyn?'

'It seems we're both on the same quest,' Rosa said, 'but from different directions.'

'Who was the coloured youth you were talking to when we came in?'

'He heard me mention Mervyn's name to the barmaid and came across and spoke to me. He wanted to know my interest in Mervyn and I'd not got beyond telling him what I've already told you when you appeared and he vanished.'

'What was his name?'

'We hadn't got as far as exchanging names.'

Sergeant Holland pursed his lips. 'Seems we must have

92

frightened him off. Pity.'

'I agree,' Rosa observed drily. 'But your resources are greater than mine and I hope you find Mervyn quickly.'

'If he exists,' Detective Constable France said, speaking for the first time.

'You've got proof of his existence,' Rosa retorted. 'The barmaid knows him. And what about the youth who's disappeared? He certainly knows him.'

'Oh, Mervyn may exist all right,' Sergeant Holland said, 'but that doesn't mean to say he's in any way connected with this murder enquiry. That part may be a figment of someone's imagination.' He gave Rosa a quietly satisfied look as though he had trumped an ace. 'Incidentally, miss, I still don't know your name.'

'Rosa Epton of Snaith and Epton.'

'I've heard of your firm,' he said in an expressionless tone. 'If you'll now excuse us, Miss Epton, we'd better get on. We've got other enquiries to make elsewhere.'

Rosa watched them depart. On their way out they paused to speak again to the barmaid.

A couple of minutes later Rosa got up to leave and also stopped to have a word with her.

'Recognise them anywhere, wouldn't you?' the barmaid remarked sardonically. 'Mind you, I'm not saying anything against them, but they do stand out like sore thumbs on Elizabeth Taylor's hands.' She gave her face another fierce sidelong peer in the mirror. 'I should know, I was once married to a copper. It just didn't work out. He was probably too good for me. That's what he thought, anyway.' She paused. 'I suppose they told you they was looking for Mervyn?'

'Yes. They seemed to doubt his existence.'

'Sometimes it's easier to believe what you want to believe.'

'That coloured boy I was talking to, has he been here before?' Rosa asked.

The barmaid shook her head. 'His was a new face to me. No prizes for guessing where he gets the money to dress like that!'

It was in a thoughtful frame of mind that Rosa returned to her car. As soon as she got back to her flat, she telephoned Colne Police Station and asked to speak to Detective Inspector Martin. She was informed that he was busy and unable to come to the phone. Could he take a message for him asked the officer on the other end of the line.

'What I really want to know is whether my client is still at the station?' Rosa said.

'I'll enquire,' the officer said politely while Rosa restrained her impatience. As if he didn't know! 'Yes, he's still here,' he said after a pause during which she heard muffled voices.

'Is he going to be released tonight?' she asked.

'I'm afraid I don't have any further information. Perhaps you'd like to have a word with Inspector Martin tomorrow.'

'Like hell I will!' Rosa muttered to herself as she put back the receiver.

She wondered how Nigel Ambrose was standing up to his interrogation and what Chief Superintendent Everson had managed to get out of him so far.

Chapter 15

When Rosa called the police station first thing the next morning she found herself put through almost at once to Inspector Martin.

'Good morning, Miss Epton,' he said in a cheerful voice. 'I was expecting you to phone. Nigel's still here helping us with our enquiries.'

Rosa always found it ominous when the police referred to her clients by their first name. It invariably indicated that a rapport had been established which could only make her own task harder in the long run.

'How much longer are you proposing to detain him?' Rosa enquired in what she hoped was a steely tone.

'Not longer than we have to,' Martin replied blandly.

'Perhaps you'd tell Chief Superintendent Everson from me that unless my client is released by this afternoon, I shall have to take legal action.'

'Of course I'll pass that on to him, Miss Epton,' Martin replied in a tone far too confident for Rosa's liking. 'There's no question of our exceeding our powers.'

'That's a matter of opinion,' Rosa said and immediately wished she hadn't. It might be a matter of opinion, but the courts would almost certainly side with the police and be against her. It all hinged on what was reasonable in the circumstances and the police had to overstretch themselves by a wide margin before being judicially castigated for unreasonable conduct. Once the police got hold of a suspect it was almost impossible to prise him out of their grip until they were ready. And that particular chapter often ended with the suspect being charged.

'I gather you've been doing a bit of sleuthing on your own, Miss Epton,' Martin remarked pleasantly.

'Looking for Mervyn, you mean?'

'Yes. It's certainly in all our interests that he should be traced.'

'The sooner the better.'

'I agree. Let's hope we run him to earth today.' After a slight pause, he added, 'Though I'm not too hopeful.'

And on that unsatisfactory note their conversation ended. For the moment there was nothing further Rosa could do and that was a situation she detested. However, sooner rather than later Nigel Ambrose would either have to be released or be charged with his uncle's murder.

'Ian didn't come home last night, Tony. His bed's not been slept in.' Denise Holtby's voice was more than usually anxious.

Her husband paused in the act of spreading marmalade on a bit of toast and looked up with a weary expression.

'He's probably spent the night at a friend's,' he said, without much endeavour to comfort. It wasn't the first time his stepson had stopped out all night without warning, but he was old enough to live his own life. The trouble was that his mother fussed over him and always had. She had spoilt him, and if she hadn't he might have caused them fewer anxieties.

'I'm so worried, Tony,' she said, still hovering in the doorway as though unable to make the effort to enter the room.

'Come and sit down and have a cup of coffee,' Tony Holtby said with a sigh. 'I expect he'll either come home or be in touch shortly.'

'And you, *chéri*, I'm worried about you, too. Something's wrong, isn't it?'

'I'm worn out by everything that's happened in the last few days,' he said in an exhausted voice.

96

'That is all?' she asked staring anxiously at him.

'Isn't it enough?'

'You promise me there's nothing else on your mind?'

He gave his head an impatient shake and turned to stare out of the window. Denise watched him with a doubtful expression. Aware that she was doing so, he picked up his piece of toast with an abstracted air and took a bite.

'What's going to happen, my darling?' she asked suddenly in a tone of impending tragedy.

He frowned and reluctantly looked in her direction.

'I don't know what you mean,' he said austerely.

She seemed about to come across the room to him, but instead, after hovering indecisively for several seconds, she turned and went upstairs.

He pushed his half-eaten piece of toast away from him and gazed moodily at his unopened newspaper.

What a ghastly strain events had put them under! Could anything ever be the same again? He had pretended not to know what she meant by her last question, but he believed he really knew quite well. What *was* going to happen? The question was real enough, only the answer remained unknown.

It was as if an iron screen had come down between them and shut off communication for the first time in their married life.

Sometimes truth could be as capriciously destructive as a hurricane, he reflected grimly as he got up from the breakfast table.

His stepson Ian had a lot to answer for.

Stephen Welford had always disliked taking work home, though this had often been necessary when he was in practice at the Bar. Even then he used to prefer to stay late in Chambers or go in early when the place was quiet and deserted. It was much the same now that he was a judge. He either stayed on in his room after everyone else had departed or arrived at an hour when most people were still having breakfast.

It had only just gone eight o'clock that morning when he drove through the gateway of Runnymede Crown Court and parked at the rear in an area reserved for judges and senior court officials. His room was next to Judge Holtby's and commanded a sweeping view of the river and the hotchpotch of weekend homes that lined the farther bank, many of which were now surrounded by water.

For a while he stared hypnotically at the swollen river flowing tirelessly past. Then he sat down at his desk and began to read the depositions in the case he was due to try that day. He didn't find it easy to concentrate and looked up constantly from his papers to stare abstractedly across the room.

He had been so looking forward to sitting at the new court and to working in harness with Tony Holtby with whom he had always got on well. He had a natural humility and frequently counted his blessings, the chief of which had been his appointment as a judge. He had thought he had probably ditched his chances as a result of his affair with Heather Ambrose. Marrying her had been a calculated risk he had gladly taken, his love of her being infinitely greater than his desire for judicial office. But now he had both and regarded himself as the luckiest man on earth; until, that is, Edmund Ambrose had cast his ugly shadow across all their lives and had set in train events that had the inevitability of a Greek drama, for Stephen Welford could see nothing but tragedy ahead.

He had been working in his room for about an hour and a half when there was a knock on the door and Leo Dodd came in.

'Hello, Leo, you're early this morning,' Welford said with a friendly smile.

'I suppose you've been here since six,' Dodd remarked.

'Not quite.'

'May I sit down?'

'Of course.'

The clerk pulled up a chair and cautiously sat down. He was clearly ill at ease and seemed reluctant to explain the reason for his visit.

'Have you heard how police enquiries are going?' Welford asked in an effort to break the ice.

'They're questioning Ambrose's nephew. He was a gate-crasher at the opening ceremony.'

'What motive is he supposed to have had for murdering his uncle?'

Leo Dodd gave him a surprised look. 'I've no idea. I thought perhaps you might know.'

'Well I don't.' After a pause he added, 'I pray he's not going to be charged. Things are bad enough for Heather and me without that.'

'If there's evidence, they'll charge him.'

'Of course they will and rightly so. I just hope there isn't any evidence to show he did it.'

The clerk gave a vague nod and let out an exaggerated sigh.

'You've obviously got something on your mind, Leo, what is it?' Welford said, once more breaking a silence.

'There's a rumour going round my office and I'll be glad of your advice, Stephen,' Dodd said, fidgeting in his chair. 'I don't know whether I should tell the police or not. It's extremely sensitive and embarrassing.' He glanced at Judge Welford who had assumed a wary expression. 'You know the police have now accounted for all the photographers who were out on the balcony save for one? This rumour concerns the missing one.'

'Well, go on.'

'It's being suggested that it was Judge Holtby's stepson,' Dodd blurted out.

'Ian Lester?' Stephen Welford said in a voice of astonishment. 'Why on earth should he want to murder Ambrose?' After a pause he went on, 'I suppose there are bound to be some wild rumours flying around, but that one's too wild for words. Anyway, where did you hear it?'

'Reg Pitt, the janitor, told a girl in my office who passed it on to me last night just as I was leaving.'

'How does Pitt come into the story?'

'His wife was one of the photographers and was standing next to Ian Lester. If, of course, it was him.'

'Has she told the police?'

Dodd shook his head. 'All she can say is that there was a slim, dark youth with a camera next to her and we know that no such person has come forward.'

'There must be a thousand slim, dark youths within a ten mile radius of this building,' Welford observed scornfully. 'Does Mrs Pitt know Ian Lester?'

Leo Dodd shook his head again.

'No, but after she'd given a statement to the police she was discussing the matter with her husband . . .'

'And he jumped to the conclusion that the missing photographer was Tony Holtby's stepson? It's a preposterous suggestion.'

'Reg Pitt has met Ian Lester.'

'Does that make it any stronger?' His tone was contemptuous.

'There is a bit more to it than that,' Dodd said with a squirm. 'Pitt thinks he saw Ian Lester's car parked near the court that morning.'

'What do you mean by *near*?'

'It was up on the verge in Ferry Lane about a quarter of a mile away.'

'And what was Pitt doing in Ferry Lane that morning?' Welford asked in a still sceptical voice.

'He'd come to court on his son's bicycle and later found it'd been stolen. Someone told him he'd seen a boy riding it down Ferry Lane and Reg went off in pursuit.'

'And did he find the bicycle?'

'No.'

'But he says he saw a car which he believes belongs to Tony Holtby's stepson?'

'Yes, a small red sports car. Old and beaten up in

appearance.'

'Did he take the registration number?'

'No, he didn't have any reason to do so. He was more interested in finding his son's bicycle.'

'I suppose he doesn't know the make either?'

'He thinks it was a Triumph, but he's not sure.'

Stephen Welford gazed out of the window in a thoughtful silence while Leo Dodd plucked nervously at his lower lip.

'What I was wondering,' he said 'was whether you might see fit to have a word with Tony Holtby before he goes into court this morning. You could enquire casually after his stepson. I mean, if it turns out he's abroad, then obviously the rumour's entirely false and should be squashed as quickly as possible . . .'

'As far as I know he's not abroad and is living at home. That's what Mrs Holtby told my wife the other day when they were talking on the phone.' He got up and began pacing the room. Eventually he said, 'You know as well as I do, Leo, that evidentially there doesn't begin to be a case. All you have is a car that might or might not be Ian Lester's and a description that could fit anyone of around the same age.'

'I realise that, but isn't it a matter for the police to look into as they see fit?'

'So why do you want me to speak to Tony Holtby first?'

'His reaction might assist one way or the other.'

'All right,' he said at length, 'I'll have a word with him in the hope of killing this silly, dangerous rumour.'

'I'd be glad if you would,' Dodd said in a tone of relief as he got up from his chair.

After the clerk had left the room, Stephen Welford fell to wondering whether Leo Dodd might not have had an ulterior motive in the approach he had just made. After all there were other rumours flying around and there was scarcely anyone attached to the court who wasn't in some way affected.

But as quickly as the thought entered his head he dismissed it. Please God, don't let him fall prey to all the rumour-mongering!

Just after ten o'clock he thought he heard Tony Holtby's door open and close and decided to go and speak to him.

He was shocked by his colleague's appearance. He looked as if he had not slept all night and he wore a haunted expression.

'Good morning, Tony,' he said in a voice as cheerful as the atmosphere permitted. 'We don't seem to have had a chance to talk the last couple of days. Everything sound and solid on your front?'

'How can anything be sound and solid with this wretched investigation hanging over our heads?'

'I know. Incidentally, I understand the police have detained Ambrose's nephew for questioning.'

'So I hear.'

'I suppose he could have done it.'

Tony Holtby gave a shrug of indifference.

'How's Denise?' Welford asked.

'As depressed as I am.'

'Any of the children at home?'

Holtby shook his head. 'Ian comes and goes,' he said vaguely. 'If you'll excuse me, Stephen, I must make a couple of phone calls before I go into court. See you later in the day, I expect.'

Welford returned to his room in a wholly unsettled state of mind. His quest had achieved no useful purpose. Indeed it had only served to increase his own morbid suspicions.

Henry Keffingham tilted back his desk chair and gazed sardonically at Inspector Martin over the top of his spectacles. Soon after he had arrived at Chambers he had received a call from the police asking if he could be available for interview some time that morning. With the sudden collapse of the drugs case he had one of his rare days out of court and was proposing to spend it on paper work. The prospect of an interview didn't displease him and he told his clerk to say they could come as soon as they wished.

Although he was not going to display any undue interest in

102

their enquiries, he was nevertheless keen to discover what progress was being made.

'Have you yet established the old boy's actual cause of death?' he asked casually.

'He died of drowning, but we're still waiting for the analyst's report on the pellet removed from his neck. It almost certainly contained ricin, but we don't yet know how much.'

Keffingham nodded judicially. 'So you won't have any difficulty sustaining a charge of murder in the circumstances. Even if the pellet contained insufficient poison to kill him outright, your chain of causation is good enough.'

'You don't think counsel could argue otherwise?'

'Oh, counsel can argue any point you care to dream up,' he said blandly. 'That's what they're paid for. But they wouldn't get far with that one.' He frowned slightly. 'But supposing the old boy hadn't done a backward somersault into the river, his life might well have been saved and that might have upset somebody's calculations, don't you think?'

'In the case of the Bulgarian defector who was poisoned by a jab in his thigh from an umbrella his condition wasn't diagnosed in time. Another Bulgarian who was attacked in a Paris street showed similar symptoms and they found this tiny pellet in his back. Had it not been for the earlier case in England, he would probably have died as well. As it was his life was saved.'

'I dare say, inspector, and the odds are old Ambrose's life would have been saved as well once they discovered the pellet in his neck.'

'I'm told, sir, that he was someone who didn't like pandering to illness and I suppose he might have assumed that it was nothing more than a sudden skin eruption which would go away as quickly as it had come. After all one doesn't imagine there are people standing around waiting to shoot poison pellets at one.'

'One will after this,' Keffingham observed drily. 'Anyway the murderer's provided you with a colourful scenario and a

103

few teasers to work on.'

'Teasers, sir?'

'Why did he choose such an elaborate and uncertain means of execution? That must be something you've been asking yourselves.'

'We have indeed,' Martin said, and left it at that.

'Anyway,' Keffingham went on after a slightly awkward pause, 'you haven't come here to ask me for my theory, so in what way can I help you?'

'I'd be very interested to hear your theory, sir.'

'Well I don't have one. Very few people will have actually mourned old Ambrose's demise, but I can't think of anyone who had sufficient animus to murder him.'

'Did you ever run foul of him, sir?'

Henry Keffingham's expression abruptly changed. 'If I'm one of your suspects, you'd better say so and this interview can proceed on a different footing.' His tone was abrasive and he glared balefully at Martin as he spoke.

Inspector Martin blinked in mild surprise and decided to bend with the wind.

'I'm sorry, sir, it was just that I'd heard a rumour . . .'

'I'm not interested in any rumours affecting myself other than, if necessary, to issue writs for defamation. I hope that makes the position quite clear.' He paused before saying, 'Was there any material matter on which you wanted my assistance?'

'I understand, sir, that you declined to take part in the photographic session on the balcony?'

'I should bloody well think so. Who'd want to be photographed in that company? Anyway, I had something more important to attend to.'

'May I ask what it was?'

'You may and what's more I'll tell you,' he said with a sudden return to affability. 'After all those interminable speeches I needed a drink; not to have my photograph taken.'

'I hope you were successful,' Martin said with a smile.

104

'Only after I'd invaded the catering manager's parlour.'

'So you saw nothing at all of what happened on the balcony?'

'It was all just starting as I made off.'

'Did you see anyone or anything to arouse your suspicions?'

'No one and nothing.'

Martin hadn't expected to get much out of the interview and was therefore not unduly disappointed by its outcome.

He had run across Henry Keffingham in a few cases and distrusted him. The interview that morning had done nothing to change his view. There was no evidence whatsoever to suggest he had any part in the judge's death, but Martin had sensed a greater interest in the police enquiries than he was disposed to reveal. And then there had been his abrupt changes of attitude from affability to hostility and half way back again.

Martin knew, of course, about his trouble in front of Mr Justice Ambrose in the civil case, but had been unprepared for such an angry reaction at the merest mention of the subject. But he had the reputation of often walking a professional tightrope, which might explain his aggressive wariness.

Blaker sat back on the sofa with the same fastidious air that characterised all his movements. He and Gail Bristow and Monty Yarfe were in his flat in Mayfair, which was situated above the fine arts shop which was both a legitimate business and a front for his less legitimate activities. Of these the drug business was by far the most profitable.

The atmosphere in the flat was relaxed and almost celebratory.

'Thank God that trial finished when it did,' Yarfe observed. 'It was driving me mad sitting there day after day listening to all those lawyers. They could make a cup final sound like a book at bedtime.'

Blaker smiled lazily. 'We'd better not use Heathrow for a

while,' he said. 'Beeston'll be out for revenge. I've never seen anyone as angry as he was at the end.'

'Unforgiving bastard,' Yarfe remarked. 'Beeston, I mean. Why can't he take the rough with the smooth?'

'Customs officers dislike losing even more than the police. Particularly if they believe somebody else has resorted to dirty work.'

'You're not going to suggest, are you, Bernie, that we stay out of business for a while?'

'Certainly not. We'll just steer clear of Beeston and his crowd at Heathrow.'

'It was a good idea our being separately defended,' Gail Bristow said, speaking for the first time.

'It was essential.'

Monty Yarfe frowned. He knew that if it had ever come to the crunch, Blaker would have sunk him without a tremor in order to save his own skin. He was the boss who made all the big decisions and who demanded total obedience from those who worked for him. He was also indisputably the brains of the outfit.

'What I have to decide now,' Blaker went on thoughtfully, 'is how we can best exploit the present situation.'

'Do we need to exploit it?' Gail asked.

'I agree; that's the first question.'

'What are we going to do about Marcus Watt?' Yarfe enquired belligerently. 'He's no longer safe to have around. I bet the police are already putting pressure on him to talk.'

'You can forget Marcus! I've made sure he's so frightened he'd hardly even dare open his mouth to buy a packet of cigarettes.'

Yarfe gave Blaker a look in which awe and surprise were blended. 'Good,' he muttered in a little boy's gruff voice.

'Now before I was interrupted,' Blaker went on smoothly, 'I was raising the question of whether we should try and exploit the present situation, and, if so, how.'

'What exactly do you mean by present situation, Bernie?' Yarfe asked with a scowl. He hadn't liked being reproved

106

and wanted to show that he was still someone to be reckoned with.

'I was referring to the police investigation into the judge's death,' Blaker said in a quietly patient tone.

'I imagined that was it,' Yarfe remarked with a self-important nod.

'I'll think about it and do what I consider best,' Blaker said, giving Gail a small wink. 'It might be a good idea to get in touch with Miss Epton.'

At that moment the phone rang and he put out a hand to answer it. For a couple of minutes he listened without interruption while the other two watched him intently.

'That's his problem,' he said in a tone that forbade any argument. 'We struck a bargain, he delivered his side and I'll keep mine. In fact I've already done more than keep mine. He should be grateful for the bonus I provided . . . No, I've no wish to see him . . . Tell him to pull himself together and stop being silly.' He dropped the receiver back on its cradle and, giving Gail a wry grimace, said, 'I definitely think I'll get in touch with Miss Epton.'

Chapter 16

Rosa had spent a fretful day waiting for news from Colne Police Station. Though she had more than enough other work to occupy her attention, her mind kept on coming back to Nigel Ambrose and his improbable story.

Normally she went from one case to the next with total concentration and it annoyed her that the judge's nephew intruded so heavily on her thoughts. She felt she should have been able to dismiss him from her mind until news of his fate reached her. He had been a client for such a short time and she had not been much taken with him at that, but there he was distracting her thoughts and generally causing her to be out of sorts with herself.

She had every intention, if she had heard nothing by the end of the day, of calling the station and finding out what was happening, but there was no point in doing so earlier. She knew that importunate calls from solicitors were liable to be counter-productive where the police were concerned. So all she could do was muster her patience and get on with other work. She wished, however, that her partner, Robin Snaith, was in the office because she could have discussed matters with him. She leaned on him heavily when a case was troubling her and he never failed to give her sound advice and, at the same time, calm her spirit. But Robin was in Manchester for three days defending a fellow solicitor who had been charged with embezzling clients' money.

It was shortly before five o'clock that her phone rang and Stephanie announced that Detective Inspector Martin was on the line.

'Good evening, Miss Epton,' he said in his usually courteous voice. 'I'm calling you on Mr Everson's instructions to let you know that Nigel Ambrose will shortly be charged with his uncle's murder. If you wish to be present, Mr Everson is prepared, as a matter of courtesy, to defer the charging until you arrive.'

'I'll come straight away,' Rosa said without hesitation.

'Then we'll wait till you get here, Miss Epton.'

Rosa disliked bad manners as much as anyone, but invariably felt a niggle of irritation when police officers stressed their own courtesy.

It took her thirty minutes to reach the police station and Inspector Martin emerged to greet her as soon as she arrived.

'He'll be detained here overnight,' he said, 'and appear before the magistrates in the morning. We shall be seeking a week's remand in custody.'

This was what she had expected and she accepted the information with a nod.

'You'll probably want to have a word with him after he's been charged and I'll be around if you wish to speak to me later.'

The charging was done by a uniformed inspector and lasted a bare couple of minutes.

Nigel Ambrose looked tired, but otherwise unconcerned. He had given Rosa a weary smile when she came into the room.

'I suppose it was inevitable,' he said, once the formalities were completed and he and Rosa were left alone for a few minutes.

'Why do you say that?' she asked with a frown.

'The culmination of a misspent life,' he said with a small, sly smile.

'Have you made a written statement?' she asked anxiously.

He nodded. 'Seemed best to tell them the truth. I told them more or less the same as I told you.'

'How much more, how much less?' Rosa asked with a sigh.

'They'll give you a copy if you ask them,' he said airily, 'and you'll see.'

'Did they put you under pressure to make a written statement?'

'Not really. On the whole they've treated me very decently. I was quite surprised.'

'But you haven't confessed to murdering your uncle?'

'Good gracious, no! Only to pointing a camera at him,' he said with an ingratiating smile.

That could be bad enough, Rosa reflected.

'How did the police seem to react to your story?' she asked.

'They questioned me closely about Mervyn and Fred.'

'Fred?' Rosa said with a puzzled expression. 'Oh yes, I remember, he was the person your uncle had sent to prison and who wanted to have a bit of harmless revenge.'

'That's right. I told them I'd never met Fred and only knew what Mervyn had said.'

'Did they seem sceptical about that part of your story?'

'A bit,' he replied with a vague shrug.

'It would have been surprising if they hadn't.'

'I know. But when you're offered a hundred pounds for almost nothing, you don't stop and ask a lot of questions. And I also got a tenner to cover my expenses. I don't think I told you that.'

If Nigel Ambrose had been set up to commit a murder, those concerned had certainly got him on the cheap. Rosa felt her only hope was to persuade a court that his story was so incredible, it had to be true. The major hurdle was going to be to convince anyone that he really believed the camera was a genuine article and not a lethal weapon.

She got up from her chair.

'I'll see you at court in the morning,' she said, 'and we'll have a further talk afterwards before you're removed to Brixton prison for the next seven days.'

'Any chance of bail?'

'Absolutely none. It's not even worth applying. But I take it you want me to ask for legal aid?'

'I haven't got any money, I'm afraid.'

Rosa assumed that the hundred pounds had gone almost as soon as he had received the two instalments.

Inspector Martin, who had been hovering in the corridor, approached as soon as Rosa emerged from the room in which she had been interviewing her client.

'Everything all right, Miss Epton?' he enquired solicitously.

Rosa ignored the question and said, 'I'd like to have a copy of his statement.'

'I'm sure there'll be no difficulty over that. I'll have a word with Mr Everson and have one ready for you in the morning.'

When the police were as obliging as that it usually meant, in Rosa's experience, that they felt their case was well buttoned-up. And yet how could they feel so confident until they could prove a motive? A specific motive, that is, as opposed to the general ill-will and resentment that Mr Justice Ambrose contrived to stir up all around him.

As if reading her thoughts, Inspector Martin now said with a note of complacence, 'I suppose Nigel told you we've been able to establish a motive.' Observing her expression he went on, 'I can see that he hasn't – '

'What motive are you talking about?' Rosa enquired, trying to hide her feelings.

'We've found a letter he sent his uncle in which he threatens him with murder. It was amongst the deceased's papers in his flat in the Temple.'

'Does it bear a date?' Rosa asked in a tone as brittle as a bowl of eggshells.

'It was posted two weeks ago.'

'May I see it?'

'I'll let you have a copy in the morning, at the same time as his statement.'

'And it actually threatens the judge with murder?'

111

'It doesn't use that precise word, but it contains an implicit threat to kill.'

Rosa let out a sigh of relief. It might be implicit in the police view, but there could still be room for argument. Nevertheless it was a nasty shock to learn that he had written his uncle a threatening letter so close to his death. And the fact that he had not mentioned it to her did nothing to increase her confidence in him as a client.

As soon as she arrived at the Magistrates Court the next morning she asked to be allowed to see him.

'Good morning, Rosa,' he greeted her cheerfully. 'Incidentally, is it all right to call you Rosa? The cells are far more comfortable than I'd expected and I'm feeling in rather good spirits. And I was given the best breakfast I've had for years.'

Anyone might think he had just learnt that he was heir to his uncle's fortune, Rosa reflected, rather than standing charged with his murder.

'I'm glad you're in such good spirits, because I'm not.'

'Why, what's happened?'

'I don't like clients who hide things from me.'

He blinked and appeared genuinely puzzled.

'What have I done?'

'Why didn't you tell me you'd sent your uncle a threatening letter only two weeks before his death?'

He looked sheepish. 'I didn't know it would be found, did I? I thought he might have destroyed it.' He paused. 'Anyway I did tell you that I'd sent him letters asking for money.'

'You didn't mention you'd sent one as recently as that.'

'I didn't think it mattered.'

'What did you put in the letter?'

'I told him I was desperate for money and surely he could send me some.'

'And?'

'I reminded him that my mother had been his favourite sister.'

112

'And?'

'I said I might be driven to do something if he turned me down.'

'Do what?' Rosa asked bleakly.

'I forget exactly what I said,' he remarked petulantly.

'Try and remember. It's important.'

'The police have got the letter. Why don't you ask to see it?'

'I have done. In the meantime, I'd like to have your recollection of the contents.'

With a resigned shrug he said, 'I think I suggested that he might have an accident.'

'What sort of accident?'

'A nasty accident.'

'You didn't by any chance say a *fatal* accident?'

'As a matter of fact, I think I did,' he said with a squirm.

And to Rosa's despair, when she later saw the letter, as a matter of fact he had.

Chapter 17

Although Nigel Ambrose's court appearance that morning was not likely to last more than a few minutes and was little more than a formality, the press turned up in force. After all, it was a rare enough occurrence for a judge of the High Court to be murdered (too rare in the view of some) and for it to have happened in such a bizarre manner helped to add to the drama of the occasion.

As soon as Ambrose appeared in the dock, the clerk read out the charge and then Inspector Martin stepped forward and asked for a week's remand in custody, saying that the police still had many enquiries to make and that their file would in due course be submitted to the Director of Public Prosecutions.

Rosa, when invited, said she had no questions to ask the officer and wished only to apply for legal aid on behalf of her client.

Thus, two and a half minutes after entering the courtroom, the defendant left it again to await transport to Brixton prison where he would spend the next seven days. Not to mention endless weeks and months ahead as the process of law inexorably coiled itself around him like a giant boaconstrictor.

Rosa had noticed Detective Chief Superintendent Everson standing against a wall while Martin was in the witness box and he came across as soon as the brief proceedings were over.

'I hope you'll believe me, Mr Everson,' she said, 'when I

say I was intending to take the initiative in telling you my client's story, but that you detained him before I had an opportunity. I did, in fact, try and see you at the Crown Court the morning after he had come to my office, but you weren't available and thereafter I was tied up in the Blaker case for most of the day.'

'If you tell me that, Miss Epton, I accept it. Though I wouldn't from some of your solicitor colleagues. Not that it makes much difference in the long run whether we found him or he came to us.'

'I've seen his statement and it's almost precisely what he told me when he sought my advice.'

'It's a rum story all right,' Everson observed.

'It could be true.'

He gave Rosa a dubious look. 'Possibly; apart from one important detail. Nobody's going to believe that he thought he had an ordinary camera.'

'How can you say that when we don't have it? It may have had the exact appearance of a genuine camera.'

'I know juries are gullible, Miss Epton, but they're not that gullible.'

'I hope you accept what he says about having been given the camera by this person called Mervyn.'

Everson pulled a face. 'I don't know about Mervyn, but I accept your client wasn't in it alone. He doesn't strike me as the sort of person who'd have been able to get hold of a weapon of that kind on his own.'

'Would you agree that he must have been used by somebody else to commit the crime?'

'If you're asking me whether I believe he was an innocent agent, the answer's an emphatic no. All I'm saying is that he probably had accomplices.'

'Mervyn, for example?'

'Possibly.'

'You'll be following up that angle?'

'Certainly.'

'I'm glad to hear that.'

Everson fixed her with a steely glance. 'Don't forget, Miss Epton, that your client recently threatened his uncle with a fatal accident and two weeks later he's dead. That's not so easy to explain away.'

'The letter's just bluster. He obviously wrote it in a mood of savage frustration.'

'Tell that to the jury!'

Rosa had the impression that Everson had talked to her more freely than he would ordinarily have done in view of the assistance she had given at the outset of his enquiries, well before Nigel Ambrose had ever appeared on the scene. But she had an even stronger impression that he was not as confident in his case as he made out. Ambrose might have had motive and opportunity and have told an outlandish story that stretched one's credulity . . . and yet several large question marks hung over supposed events.

As she drove away from court, Rosa decided it was to these that she must now address her mind.

Chapter 18

Chief Superintendent Everson was a firm upholder of old-fashioned values relating to law and order, believing in both corporal and capital punishment. Nevertheless, he couldn't help secretly regarding Mr Justice Ambrose's murderer as a public benefactor. Moreover, as Rosa had divined, the case troubled him. Although he felt he was justified in charging Nigel Ambrose, the fact remained that he had been under pressure to produce a result as quickly as possible and it had not been practicable to delay taking action.

He was still on to Martin about the missing photographer. He had to be traced in order to be eliminated from the enquiry. Who was this dark-haired youth who had vanished immediately afterwards? As long as he remained untraced, he was a distraction, an irritant, and a gift to the defence.

He also still felt there was something odd about Judge Welford's brother. He didn't somehow fit the role of family photographer and then there was the caretaker's wife who was sure he had been in possession of two cameras.

He had tried to see Barney Welford earlier, but had been unable to get in touch with him. Thereafter he had been fully occupied with Nigel Ambrose.

He decided, however, that he would now make another effort to see Judge Welford's brother. Ambrose's brief appearance in court that morning gave him a couple of hours to play with.

The address he had was of a flat on the south side of Barnes Common. He decided not to give any advance warning of his

117

arrival, but hope that his quarry would be at home. He told Detective Sergeant Luke to accompany him.

It turned out to be the ground-floor flat of a converted semi-detached. Sergeant Luke, delighted to be at his chief's side, pressed the bell marked *B. Welford*.

The door was opened by a man of about sixty. A drooping left eyelid gave him a sleepy appearance which was accentuated by the slightly frozen look to that side of his face.

'Mr Welford? I'm Detective Chief Superintendent Everson and this is Detective Sergeant Luke. May we come in?'

'I've been expecting you, but I thought you'd call first.'

'We took a chance at finding you at home,' Everson said, stepping inside.

Barney Welford closed the door and led the way into a front room which looked on to the road. It was noticeable that he walked with a limp and dragged his left foot.

'I was very glad to read that you'd made an arrest,' Welford remarked as he sat down in a high-back chair to one side of the fireplace. 'It'll be a great relief to a number of people. I'm sure my brother and Judge Holtby will feel that a large black cloud has been lifted. Now they'll be able to settle down to something approaching a normal life in that splendid new court. So long as you and your officers were prowling about the building it was quite impossible.' He gave them a small tentative smile, 'And it must be a relief to you to have made an arrest so quickly.'

'And you, Mr Welford? Has it come as a relief to you as well?' Everson enquired mildly.

Barney Welford cocked his head on one side and gave them a wary look. Before answering he glanced wistfully across at a table in the window on which lay a number of leather-bound volumes in various states of renovation.

'I'm relieved for others, my brother in particular. That's all I meant.'

'I understand you received a last minute invitation to the opening ceremony when Mrs Welford decided not to attend?'

118

'It wasn't all that last minute. About a week beforehand.'

'You've told us you were one of the photographers on the balcony . . .'

'I'm afraid my photos weren't very good. I'm not as skilful with a camera as I used to be.'

'The woman standing next to you thought you had two cameras. Did you?'

'Why on earth should I take two when I can scarcely handle one?'

'Nevertheless, that was her impression.'

'She probably mistook my hearing aid for a camera. I had one of those old-fashioned contraptions that looked a bit like one and I was using it that day. I'm now wearing one of these modern ear pieces.' He made a vague gesture towards an ear. 'It's taken me a long time to get used to it and I kept on going back to the old one.'

'May I see the other?'

'I'm afraid not. I've thrown it away.'

'Thrown it away!' Everson echoed in a surprised tone. 'That's a funny thing to have done, Mr Welford.'

Barney Welford swallowed uncomfortably.

'I knew as long as I kept it I'd probably go on using it and that if I was to persevere with this one I must get rid of the other. It's as simple as that,' he concluded in a faintly defiant tone. 'Anyway, I showed it to your Inspector Martin.'

'Where did you discard it?'

'In the dustbin.'

'Has there been a refuse collection since then?'

'Yes.'

'So it's gone for ever?'

'Presumably.'

Everson scratched his head and grimaced.

'I'd have expected you to have held it in reserve. It strikes me as extraordinary to have thrown away an expensive item like that.'

'I've told you why.'

'Can you give me particulars of its make?'

119

'I can probably find the old instruction leaflet if I look.'

He rose from his chair and limped across to a desk. He rummaged in several pigeon-holes, making increasingly exasperated sounds as he did so. At length he turned round.

'I don't seem to have it any longer,' he said bleakly. 'I suppose I must have thrown it away. I'm sorry I can't help you.' He paused and added in an aggressive voice, 'You'll have to take my word that it didn't fire poison pellets, if that's what you're thinking.'

'I'm just asking questions and listening to answers, Mr Welford,' Everson said blandly.

'Now that somebody's been charged with Ambrose's murder, I don't know why you're so interested in my hearing aid.'

Put like that, nor did Everson. And yet he was.

'Would you have any theories as to why that particular place and moment were chosen for his lordship's despatch?' he asked.

'None. Presumably his nephew decided it was the most opportune time.'

'Yes, but why?' Everson said, thinking aloud more than asking a question.

'If the person charged can't tell you, who can?'

'Oh, we have *his* explanation, but I'm still interested in other people's views.'

'I'm afraid I have none.'

It was the end of an interview that Everson could only regard as unsatisfactory. Unsatisfactory because, apart from clearing up the mystery of Welford's possession of a second camera, it had been a general fishing expedition in which nothing had been caught. He wondered if he'd mishandled the occasion. If Barney Welford did have something to hide, it still remained hidden.

'I don't believe for a moment he threw his hearing aid away,' Sergeant Luke remarked as they left the house. 'It doesn't make sense. You just don't throw out things like that as long as they've still got some use.'

'Why should he lie about it?' Everson asked a trifle wearily.

'Because he's got something to hide. It's the only explanation.'

'You realise what you're saying, don't you?'

The sergeant gave a puzzled frown. 'I don't get your drift, sir.'

'That his lordship's murderer may still be at large.'

Chapter 19

If Nigel Ambrose hadn't murdered his uncle, who had?

This was the question Rosa kept asking herself as she sat in her office later that day. She again studied the list of those who had taken photographs out on the balcony which Inspector Martin had given her (as a matter of courtesy, he had inevitably stressed) that morning. He had also told her who the various people were. She had questioned him about the one person who had not come forward and who remained unidentified.

'Of course we shall go on trying to find him, Miss Epton,' he had said reassuringly. 'It's in our interest as much as yours to do so. Otherwise I can see your counsel seeking to pin the crime on a conveniently missing person.'

'But naturally,' Rosa had replied with an elfin smile.

It was on this strangely elusive photographer that Rosa now focussed her mind. The description, such as it was, gave him as a dark-haired youth of slim build, which, as Inspector Martin had pointed out, could fit five people out of ten travelling to work on a bus any morning of the week.

The person who had provided the description was Mrs Pitt, the wife of the court janitor and Rosa decided to pay her a visit the next day. It meant a rearrangement of her work, including an appearance in the local Magistrates Court. Happily Rosa had a prized reputation of never wasting the court's time and hence the clerk invariably met her wishes in such matters. In this instance he said he would bring her case forward, so that she would be in, on and out within the opening quarter of an hour.

By eleven o'clock she was on her way to Runnymede where she arrived fifty minutes later. She had ascertained that the Pitts lived in Egham about a mile from the court. Like the police on such occasions, she favoured an unannounced visit. She hadn't wanted to be turned down on the telephone or have Mrs Pitts say that she must first speak to her husband. There was always the risk of a wasted journey, but she had to be prepared for that. Once the door was opened, she was confident of being able to inveigle her way inside, however unpromising the initial response.

Their home turned out to be a small bungalow, fronted by a trim strip of lawn and two flower beds in which a few foolhardy daffodils were making a brave showing.

Parking her car outside, she approached the mustard-coloured front door. She pressed the bell and heard a melodious chime, followed by brisk footsteps on a parquet floor.

'Mrs Pitt?' she said, when a woman in her mid-forties opened the door. She was wearing a flowered overall and a loosely knotted head scarf. She peered at Rosa with a certain amount of consternation.

'Oh! . . . Oh, I thought it was my friend.' Her hand flew up and began to remove the covering on her head, which she obviously felt diminished her dignity in front of a stranger.

'My name's Rosa Epton. I'm a solicitor . . .'

'You were at the court the other day. I remember seeing you.'

'That's right. I believe we were both on the balcony when it all happened.'

'I know. Wasn't it a shock for everyone? Particularly the poor old judge, though I gather nobody liked him. Even so I don't expect he thought it'd be his last day when he got up that morning.' She paused and removed the headscarf with a flourish, at the same time shaking her head like a dog after a roll on the grass. 'I suppose that's what you've come about. Why don't you step inside? I'll make a cup of coffee. I was

123

about to put the kettle on when you rang the bell.'

'How beautifully you keep your home!' Rosa remarked, as she looked round the living-room. 'And the garden, too!'

'It is nice, isn't it?' Mrs Pitt said complacently, warming to the flattery. 'What exactly is it you've come about?'

'I'm representing Nigel Ambrose who, as you probably know, has been charged with his uncle's murder . . .'

'Can hardly help knowing it, can one?' she said with a bit of a laugh. 'It's in all the papers and on television news as well. Did he really do it?' she went on eagerly. 'You can tell me, I won't breathe a word to anyone.'

Rosa couldn't help laughing at such an ingenuous approach.

'He says he didn't,' she remarked, 'and that's what I hope a jury will say, too. The purpose of my visit here is to ask you about the youth who was next to you on the balcony.'

'Funny he's never come forward, isn't it?' Then she added darkly, 'But perhaps it's not so funny. You know who my Reg thinks it was?' She gave Rosa a quick conspiratorial glance. 'He believes it could have been Judge Holtby's stepson. Ian something or other.'

'What makes him believe that?' Rosa asked in an intrigued voice.

'Ian whatshisname looks like the youth I saw. Trouble is I didn't take that much notice of him and can't describe him all that well, but, according to Reg, it could be him. I'll tell you what happened. Of all the days the car refused to start, it had to be that one. So Reg had to take our son's bike and because he was late, he just propped it against a wall at the side of the court. Imagine how he felt when he later discovered it had gone. Somebody told him he'd seen a youth riding it down Ferry Lane, so Reg goes chasing off there hoping to find it. He never did, but what should he see but Ian whatshisname's car parked on the grass verge about a hundred yards down.' She threw Rosa a triumphant look.

'Is he sure it was Ian's?'

'He can't swear to it, of course, because he doesn't know

124

the registration number and he had no reason to note the number of the car. He was more interested in finding Peter's bike. But he says it was exactly like Ian's car.'

'Has he reported this to the police?'

'He's told Mr Dodd who said he'd have a word with Judge Welford.'

'How does Mr Pitt come to know Judge Holtby's stepson?' Rosa enquired.

'Because the judge and his stepson came over to the court about a week before it opened and they were in the boy's car. Judge Holtby wanted to show him over the building.'

The interview was surpassing Rosa's expectations and she gazed at Mrs Pitt with a benign expression. She could even forgive her her heavily lacquered golden hair that gave her the appearance of a mass-produced doll.

'And of course since then Reg has learnt various things about young Ian whatshisname,' Mrs Pitt went on. She gave Rosa a look that clearly invited her comment.

'What sort of things?' Rosa obligingly asked.

'How he's one of those drop-outs,' she said with a smug air. 'Never had a proper job and been in trouble over drugs.'

'In trouble with the police, do you mean?' Rosa asked sharply.

'Reg said he would have been had his stepfather not been a judge,' Mrs Pitt observed not without a note of spite.

From her own professional experience, Rosa knew that the sons and daughters of well-known people were not infrequently hauled up in court for drugs offences and that, in general, the police were no respecters of persons in that context. She was also aware, however, that family position could sometimes save those only on the fringe of trouble from further action. It was therefore possible that Judge Holtby's stepson had escaped prosecution in that way.

'Do you have any idea when he was in trouble over drugs?' Rosa asked.

'I never asked Reg.'

'No reason why you should have,' Rosa said, putting down

her coffee cup and wondering how much further curiosity she could show without alienating Mrs Pitt. So far the janitor's wife had shown a complete readiness to talk without any kind of inhibition, but one question too many might cause her suddenly to switch off her flow of information. Rosa had known it to happen.

'Does your husband have any theories about the murder?' she asked in an interested voice.

'He was a bit surprised when it turned out to be the judge's nephew.'

'Nigel Ambrose has only been charged,' Rosa said firmly. 'He hasn't yet been convicted.'

'But Reg says the police never charge anyone unless they know he's done it. If the police bring a charge you can be certain he's done it, whatever the jury says. That's Reg's view.'

It was not, Rosa decided, the right moment to refute this complacent proposition with the vigour she would normally show.

'Who had been your husband's favoured suspect?' Rosa asked with a smile.

'Well, he thought it must have been this Ian whatshisname. After all, why didn't he come forward like the rest of us?'

Why not indeed, Rosa reflected, always assuming he *was* the missing photographer. And if he wasn't, who had played that mysterious role?

As she drove away, having thanked Mrs Pitt warmly for her help, she decided it was time for her to investigate Judge Holtby's stepson. If her own client had not committed the murder (and only his fragile protestation of innocence and her own instinct said otherwise) somebody else had and at the moment Ian whatshisname must be frontrunner.

As a first step she had better find out exactly what was his name.

Chapter 20

The first thing Rosa did when she returned to the office early that afternoon was to enquire when her partner was expected back.

'He's in now,' Stephanie said, 'but he has a client with him.'

'Let me know when he's free!'

Stephanie nodded. 'He wanted to be told when you came in, too,' she remarked. 'So you can look forward to a grand reunion.'

Rosa laughed. Stephanie was the most efficient telephonist-cum-receptionist any office could want. She was a willowy blonde with a thin face, a pair of cool grey eyes and a turned-down mouth. And she wore a perpetually sardonic expression.

About twenty minutes later, Rosa's phone gave a brief buzz and Stephanie said, 'He's free now.'

Robin Snaith greeted her with a friendly smile as she came into his room and flopped down in his still warm visitor's chair.

'We don't seem to have met recently,' he observed. 'Though the newspapers have as usual kept me abreast of your activities.'

He had been in practice on his own when Rosa joined the firm as an outdoor clerk. She had proved so competent and valuable that he had had no hesitation in encouraging her to qualify as a solicitor and thereafter stay with his firm. At the earliest possible moment he had offered her a partnership and had never regretted the decision. The newly-named firm of Snaith and Epton had prospered and was now one of the busiest for its size in West London. He was proud of Rosa's achievement and perfectly happy that she seemed to get the more headline-making cases. He continued to keep an unobtrusive eye on her and was always ready to offer advice when it was sought and sometimes when it wasn't.

'I want your advice, Robin,' Rosa now said. 'Are you in a good listening mood?'

'Certainly. I'll tell Stephanie not to put through any calls.'

They knew that, with that injunction, they were safe from interruption. Stephanie was firm and unflappable on such occasions.

For twenty-five minutes Robin listened while Rosa retailed everything that had happened since the opening ceremony at Runnymede Crown Court.

'I can answer one of your queries,' he said when she reached the end. 'The name of Tony Holtby's stepson is Ian Lester.'

'How do you know that?' she asked in surprise.

He cast her a faintly mocking glance. 'There was life of sorts before Rosa Epton joined the firm.'

Rosa grinned. 'I'm always forgetting that.'

'I used to brief Tony Holtby quite a bit before he became a judge and he'd talk about his family. Lester's father was a diplomat and left his wife, who is the present Mrs Holtby, before Ian was born. I seem to remember Holtby saying that he retired early from the foreign service and settled in America. But presumably none of that has any bearing on present events.' He paused and stared thoughtfully at a coloured print of old London that hung on his wall. It showed the river and a pleasant view of the Temple and its gardens. He always referred to it as his peaceful picture. 'What strikes me as the most remarkable feature,' he said at length, 'is the haphazard nature of the murder compared with the careful planning that must have preceded it. The weapon, assuming it was a disguised camera, was cunning and sophisticated, but at the same time wholly unreliable as a means of killing. In fact the odds are that it wouldn't have killed old Ambrose had he not gone into the river and been drowned. And the murderer couldn't have foreseen that would happen. So why didn't he shoot him in the orthodox way? He could have armed himself with a small revolver and fired from inside his pocket. He could still have made his escape in the ensuing turmoil.' Rosa waited as he frowned in concentrated thought. 'And if somebody really wanted to kill him, why choose such a bizarre setting for the crime? Why not murder him in his flat or when he was out for a walk? Why, in fact, should the murderer have made things so much more difficult for himself than was necessary?'

'You tell me,' Rosa said with a sigh.

'You mentioned that you wondered if he was the right target. But what I've just said would apply whoever was the intended victim. There must have been surer ways of despatching an intended victim standing on that balcony, so why that particular place and time?'

'So what's the answer?' Rosa said in a coaxing tone.

'The answer is that murder wasn't the prime motive,' he replied, giving her a challenging look.

Rosa blinked in surprise. 'If somebody didn't mean to kill him what did they intend to do?'

'Frighten him. Upset him. Give him the shock of his life.'

'In fact, what Mervyn told Nigel Ambrose.'

'Exactly. I've no idea who Fred was, but he obviously intended something more than a bit of harmless revenge. He wanted the old boy to have the most disagreeable experience of his life. Something he'd never forget. My guess is that had he not been killed, there'd have been a follow-up of some sort. An anonymous letter telling him to heed a warning *or*. After all, as I've said, nobody could have foreseen he was going to fall into the river and drown. Nigel Ambrose's instructions were merely to let his Uncle Edmund see him there with a camera. Neither he nor Mervyn nor the mysterious Fred knew there'd be a photo call out on that

129

balcony.'

'That means Nigel could have told the truth.'

'Don't sound so surprised! Clients sometimes do.'

'So who is Fred?'

'Ah! All we can do at the moment is speculate about Fred. My guess is that he's a fairly big-time criminal. Somebody with money and resources. And quite definitely somebody with a deep grudge. Probably a real psychopath. He's certainly no small-time crook, that's for sure.'

Rosa was thoughtful for a while. 'Mr Justice Ambrose must have sent hundreds of people to prison who answer that description.'

'If not thousands.'

'So where do I begin?'

'You certainly can't check on every case he ever tried. You'd need an army of researchers before you even came up with a short list of possibles. I think you should have a further stab at finding Mervyn.'

'Don't forget the police are also looking for him!'

'How strenuously, I wonder?' he said in a doubtful voice.

'And what about the missing photographer?' Rosa said after a pause. 'Where does he fit in?'

'If it was Tony Holtby's stepson, he'd have every reason not to come forward.'

'Why?'

'Because I'd surmise he was there for some reason of his own, about which he wouldn't want to be questioned in view of his stepfather's position.'

'I can't think what sort of reason it could have been,' Rosa observed.

'Nor can I at the moment, but that doesn't mean there wasn't one. He doesn't sound a very stable member of society so it might have been anything. At all events he fled when things turned out as they did.'

'That might explain the expression on Judge Holtby's face in one of the photographs,' Rosa said slowly. 'He had a startled look as though he'd just seen somebody he wasn't

130

expecting to.'

'You didn't mention that the police had shown you the photographs,' Robin remarked.

'They didn't,' Rosa said with a sheepish grin. 'I had a quick look at them when Inspector Martin left me alone in his room for a few minutes.'

Robin laughed. 'How very careless of Martin! Anyway, as you say, the expression in the photograph you saw could be explained by Ian Lester's unheralded intrusion on the festivities.'

'But it doesn't explain why he was there.'

'One can only speculate; and not very profitably.'

'What also bothers me, Robin, is that there wouldn't appear to be any link between Nigel Ambrose and the missing photographer, whoever he was.'

'I agree that they appear to be two entirely different horses in the same race.'

'Running neck and neck, would you say?'

'I know which my money would be on.'

'Nigel Ambrose, ridden by Mervyn and trained by Fred.' Robin nodded and Rosa let out a heavy sigh. 'So where do I begin?'

As if to answer her question, the phone on Robin's desk buzzed and he reached for the receiver.

'It's for you,' he said.

'I'm sorry to interrupt, Rosa,' Stephanie said in an exasperated tone, 'but he simply refuses to go away until I've put him through. It's Mr Blaker. I've told him you were engaged and couldn't speak to anyone and that I'd get you to call him later, but he insists on talking to you now. I've never known such a client,' she concluded with untypical petulance.

'That's all right, Stephanie, you can put him through. Robin and I had more or less finished anyway.'

'Miss Epton? It's Bernard Blaker. I'd very much like to see you as soon as possible. Would this evening be convenient?' Before Rosa could reply he went on, 'I could pick you up at home around seven o'clock and take you off for a drink at a quiet place I know. That should be pleasanter than talking in your office.'

Rosa was momentarily silenced by the unexpectedness of the suggestion.

'What is it you want to see me about, Mr Blaker?' she asked warily.

'I'll tell you that when we meet. Shall we say seven o'clock then? I have your address.'

Chapter 21

For the life of her Rosa couldn't think afterwards why she had agreed to such an unusual meeting. She rarely mixed business with pleasure and Bernard Blaker was the last person on earth with whom she would normally wish to go out socially. But she had the feeling she had been given no choice in the matter; except that this was absurd as she could easily have pleaded another engagement or have said firmly that he must make an appointment to see her in the office.

She could only attribute her compliance to the fact that she was intrigued to find out why he wanted to talk to her so urgently. It was the unexpectedness of his call coupled with his total confidence that she would fall in with his wishes.

When she said all this to Robin, he merely smiled. From the sound of him Bernard Blaker was not the sort of client with whom Rosa could have become emotionally involved. It was invariably amoral young men who caused her temporarily to lose her judgement and from whose dubious charms he had on occasions felt obliged to try and rescue her.

At seven o'clock that evening Rosa was still wondering what had possessed her when her answer-phone rang. She took a quick look out of the window and saw the familiar Mercedes parked in the street below.

'I'll be down in a couple of minutes,' she said a trifle breathlessly. She certainly wasn't going to have him come up to her flat.

He was standing on the pavement beside the car when she emerged and opened the rear door for her. He then went round and got in the other side. The driver was the same man who had brought him to court each morning and fetched him again at the end of the day's proceedings. He wore a dark grey suit but no headgear. Without a word he started up the engine and pulled away from the kerb as soon as Blaker closed his door.

'Do you know the Pastel Club, Miss Epton?' Blaker enquired as they drove off. Rosa shook her head and he went on, 'I've never yet met anyone who did, which is something of an advantage. It's off Park Lane. It's small and quiet which is more than one can say for most clubs.' He paused and shot her a sidelong glance. 'I really wanted to find an opportunity of thanking you in civilised surroundings for all the work you put into my case.'

Rosa gave a brief smile of acknowledgement, though she was quite sure this was not the true purpose of his seeking her company.

For the rest of the journey they made desultory conversation as she more than ever wondered what on earth she was doing in his car.

The entrance to the Pastel Club was so discreet as to be almost invisible. The decor within was a blend of pastel colours which must have cost a fortune. The lighting was indirect and came from concealed panels which cast a glow on to tinted mirrors.

'What would you like to drink?' he enquired when they were seated on a pale green banquette in a deep alcove. In front of them was a low glass table with a bowl of fresh spring flowers in the centre.

'I'd like a glass of dry white wine, if I may.'

'Certainly you may. But are you sure you wouldn't like something more exotic? The barman mixes the most original cocktails.'

Rosa shook her head. 'Just a glass of wine please.'

Blaker ordered himself a Russian vodka on the rocks.

Their drinks arrived and Rosa took a sip of her wine which was cold and delicious and far superior to what she bought for herself at the off-licence.

Blaker put down his glass and gave her a thoughtful look. 'Even though my case is over, I'm still intrigued to know what happened on that opening day,' he said. 'Have they got the right chap for the judge's murder, do you think?'

'I hope not. He's my client.'

'So I gather. He's a lucky man.'

'Being charged with murder?'

He gave her the smile he obviously felt was expected of him. 'Having you defend him is what I mean. I don't suppose I should ask you this, but do you have a strong case?'

'It's too soon to know, but I hope so.'

'I've always been fascinated by murder. Both the motives and the means. Mind you, the abolition of the death penalty has removed much of the excitement of a good murder trial. I know one shouldn't say that, but it's true. And so many murders nowadays lack finesse, but not Mr Justice Ambrose's. There was nothing crude about that. It was both subtle and ingenious.'

'You almost sound as if you'd have been proud to have committed it yourself,' Rosa remarked drily.

She had been surprised by the turn of conversation and still couldn't believe he had invited her out merely to discourse about murder.

'Has it occurred to anyone that Judge Holtby may have been the intended victim?' he asked earnestly, as though he hadn't heard her comment.

'What makes you say that?' Rosa asked warily.

'There was obviously something wrong with the poor man. He looked like someone who'd had a miraculous escape, but wondered for how long. Of course I wasn't there when it all happened, but I gather he was standing next to Mr Justice Ambrose and . . . well, one judge looks much like another when they're dressed up, particularly when seen through the viewfinder of a camera.' He put his head on one side and gave Rosa a speculative gaze.

'It's an interesting theory,' she said in the same cautious

135

tone, still wondering if this was all he had wanted to say to her. And if so, why?

The barman came up and replenished their drinks, apparently unbidden. The service in the Pastel Club was clearly as smooth and discreet as everything else about the place.

He was about to speak again when Rosa became aware of somebody who had followed the barman over and was still standing at their table. She glanced up to see a young man wearing an open neck shirt and a pale blue pullover, who was looking at Blaker with an anxious expression.

'Go away,' Blaker said in a tone as coldly angry as it was quiet.

The young man seemed about to speak when Blaker stood up and quickly escorted him across the room.

'I apologise for that interruption,' he said on his return a couple of minutes later. 'He had no right to come looking for me here and I told him so.'

It was not long afterwards that he indicated his desire to leave and Rosa got up.

As the doorman let them out, he bent his head forward and stammered in an embarrassed voice, 'I'm terribly sorry about that, Mr Blaker, but Mr Lester said you were expecting him.'

Chapter 22

Blaker insisted on sending Rosa home in the Mercedes, but asked that she should excuse him accompanying her, saying that his flat was within walking distance of the Pastel Club.

'Douglas will take you to your door,' he said as he bade her good night.

It was obvious that the incident in the club had considerably annoyed him and was the cause of their meeting being cut short. Not that this bothered Rosa who could hardly wait to get home and call Robin.

'It must have been Ian Lester,' she said as soon as she had told him what had happened. 'And I've never seen anyone look so venomous as Blaker did. But how does it all fit together, Robin?'

'It's interesting he suggested that Tony Holtby might have been the intended victim. It could be that Lester meant to kill his stepfather and did, in fact, get the wrong person. It seems clear that Tony Holtby recognised him on the balcony, hence the expression on his face you noticed in one of the photographs. But heaven knows how Lester and Blaker fit together!'

'It must be a drugs connection of some sort.'

'Possibly.'

'It's the only explanation.'

'What are you proposing to do now, Rosa?'

'Have an early night.'

'I meant next.'

'Find out everything I can about Ian Lester. In particular

what motive he could have had for killing his stepfather.'

Rosa was in court the next morning and didn't get back to her office until after lunch.

'Somebody's been trying to get you on the phone all morning,' Stephanie said on her return. 'Somebody called Mervyn. If he has another name, he didn't tell me.'

'Did he leave a number?' Rosa asked with quickening interest.

'He left nothing. He just said he was Mervyn and would call back and went on saying it each time he came through.'

'What did he sound like?'

'He had a voice like thick molasses.'

Rosa smiled. 'Well, put him through as soon as he calls again,' she said. 'If he's the person I think he is, he probably looks like molasses as well.'

It was late afternoon, however, before Stephanie announced that Mervyn was on the line, by which time Rosa had begun to wonder if he had had second thoughts about calling her.

'Miss Epton? I'm Mervyn. I'm told you were looking for me the other evening. Right?' His voice was just as Stephanie had described, deep-pitched and seductive.

'If you're the Mervyn who frequents the Queen's Head in Kilburn, yes, I was looking for you.'

He chuckled. 'I thought I'd save you the trouble of looking again. You're a lawyer, aren't you, Miss Epton?'

'Yes. I wanted to speak to you on behalf of a client.'

'Nigel?'

'Yes.'

'I'm sorry he's in trouble.'

'Then I hope you'll help him.'

He chuckled again as though the prospect amused him. 'I'm listening, Miss Epton.'

'Did you lend him a camera and tell him to take photographs at the opening ceremony of Runnymede Crown Court?'

'Go on, Miss Epton.'

138

'Were you asked to do that by someone called Fred who wanted to frighten the judge?'

This time he chuckled even more as though the memory was hilarious.

'Fred's a bit of a nutter. Gets funny ideas about people and likes to show them who's boss.'

'What's Fred's other name?'

'It's something like Smith, I think.'

'And where does he live?'

'London.'

'That should make him easy to trace,' Rosa remarked, while Mervyn had another chuckle. 'What's happened to the camera you lent Nigel?'

'How do I know, Miss Epton? He never returned it.'

'But he says he gave it to someone who came to the Queen's Head to collect it on your behalf.'

'He probably told you that to get himself out of trouble.'

'That doesn't make sense.'

'Too bad, Miss Epton.'

'Would you be prepared to meet me?'

'That might be difficult.'

'Why? I thought you wanted to help Nigel.'

'It's better we don't meet, Miss Epton.'

'Would you come to court if necessary to help Nigel?'

'I can't help him more than I'm doing.'

'If I may say so, you're not helping him at all.'

'Then that's too bad, Miss Epton,' he said in a tone free of any chuckle. 'Perhaps you'd like me to ring off.'

'No, don't do that!' Rosa cried out. 'I've got some more things to ask you. Did you ever see the photograph that Nigel is supposed to have taken?'

The chuckle returned. 'No. Fred forgot to put a film in the camera. I told you he was a bit of a nutter.'

'Was the idea simply to frighten the judge?'

'Is that what Nigel says?'

'Yes.'

'Then I'd believe him.'

139

'Who supplied the hundred pounds Nigel received?'

'Fred. Money's nothing to him.'

'Did you get anything out of it?'

'Perhaps.'

Rosa was beginning to wonder how much longer she could keep the conversation going and whether there was a great deal of point in doing so. And yet she was loth to let him go, seeing that she had no way of ever getting in touch with him again.

'Do you realise that Nigel could be wrongly convicted of murder unless you come forward?' she said a trifle desperately.

'People of my colour are wrongly convicted all the time, but nobody gets upset.'

'I should if you were my client.'

'You know something, Miss Epton, I actually believe you.'

'Then will you help me?'·

'I am helping you, Miss Epton. Didn't I call you?'

'Yes, and I appreciate it, but I'm sure you could help me a lot more if we could meet. You name the time and place and I'll be there,' she added urgently.

'I've given you all the help I can.'

'But don't you see how important it is to Nigel that you should come forward?'

'I'll think about it.'

'Is there any way I can get in touch with you?'

'No.'

'Do you know anyone called Ian Lester?' Rosa asked frantically, feeling that she was going to lose him at any moment.

There was a slight pause before he said, 'Ian Lester? Don't know him.'

'He's the stepson of a judge at Runnymede Crown Court.'

'Still don't know him.' In a distinctly wary tone he added, 'What judge?'

'Judge Holtby.'

'Oh, the one Nigel was supposed to give a fright to!'

'That was Mr Justice Ambrose,' Rosa said in a puzzled voice.

'No, it was Holtby. Holtby who put old Fred away for ten years.'

'But Nigel was Mr Justice Ambrose's nephew, not Judge Holtby's.'

'Can't help whose nephew he was. Holtby was the judge he was to give a friendly shock to.'

'You must be wrong . . .'

'I'm not wrong, Miss Epton. It's Nigel who's confused.'

'It's terribly important that we meet,' Rosa said in a pleading tone. She found herself, however, talking to a dead line. Mervyn had rung off.

Chapter 23

Judge Holtby arrived home shortly after five o'clock. Denise, who had been impatiently awaiting his return, immediately began to fuss over him. She fetched him tea, only to find he had already got himself a large whisky.

'Darling,' she cried out in dismay, 'you always have a cup of tea when you get home. It's not good to start drinking whisky so early.'

'I need a pick-me-up,' he said flatly.

Denise fluttered about him talking non-stop while he sat morose and withdrawn.

'Tony, what is wrong? I'm so worried for you.'

He gave a shrug. 'Is Ian in?' he asked.

She shook her head. 'I'm so worried about him, too.'

And with reason, he thought, though he refrained from saying so.

'Darling, go upstairs and lie down and I will wake you when it is time for a drink and dinner. You haven't slept well for nights. You have been so restless.'

'I'm going out shortly.'

'Out? Where are you going?' she asked anxiously.

'I have to meet somebody.'

'Who are you going to meet, darling? Is it to do with work?'

He nodded. 'Yes.'

'How long will you be out?'

'Maybe an hour.'

She gazed at him in consternation. Then blinking away a

tear, she hurried from the room.

It was while she was up in their bedroom that she heard him leave the house and walk round to the garage. She hastened across to the window in time to observe him drive off.

What had happened to her Tony? What was happening to their marriage? She felt close to total despair, but had no idea how to resolve the frightening tangle which enmeshed them.

Ian Lester was sitting in his car which was parked just off the road when he saw his stepfather drive past. It was about half a mile from home and he had stopped because he was in no mood to return and face one of his mother's interrogations. His brief life as an adult had always been something of a mess, but now it was even worse. Messes could usually be cleared up, but he felt things had gone beyond that. He knew he ought not to have approached Bernard Blaker in the Pastel Club, but he just had to try and see him. And now, of course, Blaker was furious with him. In fact he had never before seen anyone in such a frightening temper, the more so for being utterly controlled. And when Bernard Blaker was displeased (to put it at its mildest) it was as well to remain invisible.

Almost without conscious thought he started up the engine and set off behind his stepfather. Anything that postponed his arrival home was to be welcomed and here was a diversion with an air of mystery about it.

At first he thought his stepfather must be on his way to London to attend some function or other. Obviously not social or Denise would be with him. Probably a judges' meeting. It soon became apparent, however, that he was neither headed for the capital nor for Runnymede Crown Court. He was driving at a leisurely speed like somebody out for a family spin on a Sunday afternoon, which was surprising as his stepfather was normally a fast driver.

Lester kept the car in front in sight, but made no attempt to close the gap between them. He thought that if his stepfather looked in his rear-view mirror he must have seen a

143

battered red sports car tailing along behind, but if so, he didn't appear to connect it with his stepson.

It was a country road which wound its way through woods and green fields for several miles and which was notorious for police speed traps. Suddenly rounding a bend, Lester found that the cream-coloured Volvo had disappeared. He accelerated, imagining that his stepfather had spotted him and put on a turn of speed. After driving for the best part of a mile, he decided to turn round, now sure that the Volvo had turned off the road somewhere. Indeed he had noticed a track leading into a wood soon after his stepfather's car had vanished.

When he reached the point on his return ride, he parked and got out. He now observed fresh tyre marks where the car had traversed the muddy verge.

If Judge Holtby was keeping some secret rendezvous in a wood, his stepson was intent on finding out with whom. He even managed a small smile as he set off up the track; after all there might be a situation he could exploit to his own advantage. He had never much liked his stepfather, his mother being the only person in his life who mattered. It was to her he always ran when in trouble and she who had rescued him from trouble on more than one occasion.

It was with a furtive step and a mind full of confusingly devious thoughts that he passed through the outer fringe of trees and entered the wood.

P.C.s Bishop and Sidwell sat in their white police car waiting for prey. They had been parked for quite a while and had begun to feel deprived. Conversation was wilting. They had discussed Mrs Bishop's pregnancy and P.C. Sidwell's archery, which were their current topics of interest, and were each yawning when a red sports car shot past the farm entrance in which they were parked out of view of the road. With a combined soft satisfied sigh they set off in pursuit.

It was their perfect sort of prey, an old battered sports car and a young driver. With luck they'd get him for the lot. No driving licence, no insurance and an expired road fund certificate. Moreover it shouldn't be difficult to find a fair number of faults with the car itself. If not its brakes, then its tyres, or failing these, its steering and lights. No car could look like that and be wholly roadworthy.

Within a few hundred yards they had come up behind it, siren going and "Stop" sign flashing. The driver, however, appeared to take no notice as he sped ahead of them.

'We'll have him for reckless, as well as speeding,' P.C. Bishop remarked keenly as he sought to overtake, but failed.

A little farther on, however, the police car with its greater power and manoeuvrability managed to get past and P.C. Sidwell motioned the driver to pull in and stop.

They had barely come to a halt when the other car squeezed past and accelerated away.

'The young bugger!' Bishop remarked with a mixture of eagerness and annoyance. 'Just wait till we get him.'

Before long the road widened and became straight for about half a mile. By this time the red sports car had taken up a centre position so that nothing could pass it. But when an oncoming car caused it to swerve back to its own side, P.C. Bishop managed, with considerable skill and dexterity, to get past and pull up at an angle so as to block the road both ways.

P.C. Sidwell leapt out and ran back to the sports car.

'You're under arrest,' he shouted, wrenching open the door and seizing the driver's arm.

'Let me go! Please! Something terrible's happened,' Ian Lester said breathlessly and began to sob.

'You're bloody right it has,' Sidwell remarked grimly. 'Let me see your licence and insurance. The lot.' As he spoke he leaned forward and removed the ignition key. 'For a start, what's your name?'

'Lester.'

'Something Lester or Lester something?'

'Ian Lester. But I must get home. My stepfather's had an accident. He's dead.'

'What's he saying?' P.C. Bishop said, arriving at his colleague's side.

'That his stepfather's dead.'

'So's mine!'

'What's your stepfather's name?'

'Judge Holtby.'

The two officers exchanged a quick glance. 'Isn't he a judge at the new Crown Court?' Sidwell said, with a slight note of wariness.

'Yes. He's dead I tell you.'

'Where's he dead?'

'In his car. It's parked in a wood.'

'What wood?'

'About two miles back along the road.'

There was a moment's silence, then P.C. Sidwell said, 'You're in enough trouble already, so I hope for your sake that you're telling the truth. If this is some sort of joke, we'll also do you for giving false information and wasting police time.'

'Not to mention obstruction and trying to pervert the course of justice,' P.C. Bishop added. He was an officer who relished squeezing the maximum number of charges out of every incident.

Ian Lester shook his head numbly. 'I want to go home,' he said miserably.

'Home to your mummy, eh!' Bishop said contemptuously, unaware of the appositeness of his comment.

After a further slight pause, Sidwell said, 'Come on, out you get! You're going to show us where this body is. We'll leave your car here.' Keeping a firm grip on Lester's arm he escorted him to the police car and shoved him into the back. 'No funny business or you'll be sorry you were ever born.'

It took them five minutes to reach the track leading into the wood. The police car lurched and bounced its way between the trees until the track suddenly broadened and petered out. Ahead of them was the rear of a cream-coloured Volvo.

146

'That the car?' Sidwell asked.

'Yes.'

'Your stepfather's?'

'Yes.'

The officer got out and walked up to the driver's door. For several seconds he peered into the interior of the car, at times shading his eyes in order to see better. Then he walked round the front of the car to the other side and did the same thing.

When he came back to the police car, he said in a shaken voice, 'There's a man in the driver's seat. Looks as if he's blown his brains out.' Giving Lester a thoughtful glance he added, 'Or had them blown out by somebody else.'

Within an hour of learning of the circumstances of Judge Holtby's death, Detective Chief Superintendent Everson and Detective Inspector Martin had arrived at the station where Ian Lester was being detained.

Meanwhile a woman police inspector, accompanied by a male colleague, had gone to the Holtbys' house to break the news of her husband's death to Denise and to inform her, in as unalarming terms as possible, of her son's whereabouts. Before they had completed their mission a doctor had arrived at the house and Denise had been placed under sedation.

All she had been able to tell the officers midst bouts of uncontrollable weeping was that her husband had left home around a quarter to six, saying that he had to meet someone. He had not told her who or where and she was at a loss to explain what he was doing in his car parked in a wood four miles from home. It was at this point that hysterics had overwhelmed her and the doctor had been sent for.

The woman police inspector who had knowledge of the whole background of the matter had the brainwave to call Heather Welford who said she would drive over immediately.

The two officers arrived back at the station about half an hour after Everson and Martin reached there, and Martin left the room where Ian Lester was being interviewed to receive their report. On his return to the room he took Everson on one side and told him what Denise had said about her husband's movements.

'Who the hell would he be meeting in the middle of a wood?' Everson said, before adding, 'unless it was sonny, who's sitting here.'

He went back to his chair across the table from where Ian Lester was slumped in an attitude of resigned misery.

'So let's go through it once more,' he said grimly. 'And this time I want the truth.'

'I've told you the truth . . .'

'We'll see.' He leaned forward resting his arms on the table and thrusting his head menacingly towards the youth on the other side. 'So you're sitting parked in your car less than a mile from home, is that right?'

'Yes.'

'Why?'

'I've already told you. I didn't feel in the mood to go home.'

'Why not?'

'Because I knew my mother would ask me questions.'

'What sort of questions?'

'Where I'd been and things like that.'

'Any reason for not telling her?'

'I just wasn't in the mood.'

'You mean, you had something to hide from her?'

'No, I just didn't want to be asked questions, that's all.'

'Do you get on well with your mother?'

'I love her.'

'And yet you didn't want to go home and face her?'

'No.'

'You weren't worried about facing your father?'

'No. I didn't even know if he'd be at home.'

'Or perhaps you knew he wouldn't be?' Lester frowned and Everson went on, 'Knew he wouldn't be because you were going to meet him in that wood?'

'No, no. Why should I meet him there?'

'Now that's a really interesting question to which, sooner or later, you're going to give me an answer. Anyway, let's move on. You suddenly see your stepfather's car go by and

149

on the spur of the moment you decide to follow him, correct?'

'Yes.'

'Why?'

'I've already told you, it was something to do.'

'That's what you want me to believe?'

'It's the truth.'

'How far were you proposing to follow him?' Inspector Martin broke in.

'I don't know . . . I just wanted to see where he was going.'

'Supposing he had driven all the way to London, would you have followed him there?'

'No.'

'How far would you have gone?'

'I've no idea,' Lester said with a helpless shrug. 'Following him was just a diversion.'

'Do you think he spotted you on his tail?'

'Possibly.'

'Surely he must have done?'

'OK, probably.'

'And yet he drove on?'

'Yes.'

'Which seems to indicate,' Everson remarked, 'that he wasn't surprised to see you following him. In other words he was expecting you to do so because you had an arrangement to meet in the wood. That's the truth, isn't it?'

'No. Definitely not.'

'Anyway, after you'd lost sight of his car you turned round and retraced your steps and concluded that he'd taken the track into the wood?'

'Yes.'

'You were determined to find him, weren't you? Even on your own story, that is?'

'I wanted to discover what he was up to.'

'What did you suspect?'

'That he was meeting somebody.'

'A judge meeting somebody in the middle of a wood?' Martin enquired with eyebrows raised incredulously.

'It may sound strange, but my stepfather had been behaving very oddly recently.'

'In what way?'

'He seemed exceptionally depressed and preoccupied.'

'Would that be since the opening of the court?'

'Yes.'

'At all events, you left your car at the end of the track and proceeded on foot?' Everson said.

'Yes.'

'Tell us what happened next.'

'I've already told you.'

'Tell us again!'

'He suddenly saw me. First he looked surprised, then angry . . .'

'How far from the car were you at that stage?'

'Five or six yards.'

'And what was his position?'

'He was sitting in the driver's seat staring straight ahead. He must have heard me because he suddenly turned his head.'

'Yes, go on!'

'We just stared at one another for what seemed ages and then I began to walk closer to the car.' His voice began to tremble. 'It was then I noticed he had a shotgun between his legs. It was pointing upwards and the muzzle was a few inches from his face.' Ian Lester closed his eyes and bit his lip. 'I realised what he was going to do and I was terrified. He gave me a funny look and then he bent his head forward and there was an explosion. I just turned and fled.'

'Did you ever touch the car door?'

'I don't think so.'

'You must remember whether you did or not.'

'I'm certain I didn't.'

'Quite certain? We'll be checking the handle for fingerprints and should we find yours . . .'

'I don't remember,' he said in a scared tone.

'If you realised your stepfather was about to shoot himself,

151

why didn't you try and stop him?'

'My mind wouldn't function properly. All I could think of was to run away.'

'So you returned to your car, is that right?'

'Yes,' he said in a whisper.

'Not knowing whether your stepfather was alive or dead?'

'I knew he was dead.'

'How did you know?'

'His face was a mass of blood.'

'Is that something you've just remembered?'

'No. He couldn't have been alive. He'd shot himself at point blank range.'

'At all events you didn't bother about first aid?'

'I just wanted to get help.'

Everson let out a soft sigh.

'Is that what was uppermost in your mind, getting help?'

'Yes,' Ian Lester murmured eagerly.

'So what did you do when you found a police car behind you?'

'I panicked.'

'Panicked? But there was the very help you were looking for.' When there was no reply, Everson pressed the point again. 'Well, wasn't it?'

'I suppose so, but my mind was in such a turmoil, I didn't know what I was doing.'

'I'll tell you exactly what you were doing. You were driving like a maniac and doing your best to avoid being stopped by police. Why?'

'I've told you, I lost my head.'

'Was that because you had played some part in your stepfather's death and your only concern was to get away from the scene undetected?'

'No, no, that's not true.'

Inspector Martin now said in an insinuating tone, 'I suspect you did go right up to the car and even opened the door and that you tried to wrest the gun from him and in doing so it went off. Was that what happened?'

152

'No. I did go up to the car, but I never opened the door. He pulled the trigger before I could do anything.'

'Did you call out to him?'

'I shouted, "For God's sake, don't do it, Tony!"'

'Did he make any reply?'

'No. He just stared at me as if . . .'

'As if, what?'

'As if . . . I don't know how to put it. As if he was glad I was there to witness his death. It was a horrible look he gave me.'

'Did you ever see anyone else while you were in the wood?' Everson asked.

'No.'

'So if your stepfather had gone to meet somebody the person never turned up?'

'Yes.'

'Unless, of course, it was you.'

'I've told you it wasn't me,' Lester shouted in frustration.

'I know you have, but you haven't convinced me. What sort of terms were you on with your stepfather?'

'We got on all right.'

'Never quarrelled?'

'No.'

'Devoted to each other?'

'No.'

'What then?'

'We lived on sort of neutral terms.'

'What was your last job, Ian?' Martin asked.

'I worked in a supermarket.'

'As what?'

'General dogsbody.'

'When did you quit that?'

'About four months ago.'

'And what have you lived on since then?'

'My mother's helped me,' he said uncomfortably.

'Not your stepfather?'

'I've never asked him for anything,' he said defiantly.

'The police picked you up for drugs once, didn't they?'

'So what? Everyone smokes a bit of pot sometime or other. Anyway you can't prove anything.'

'He's getting aggressive,' Everson remarked, 'and I don't care for his attitude.'

'I'm fed up with all your questions. You've got nothing against me and you've no right to go on pestering me.'

'Nothing against you?' Everson said in a voice of astonishment.

'Apart from a few silly motoring offences.'

'I doubt whether the court will consider them silly. But be that as it may, tell me more about your relationship with your stepfather. Did he ever tell you to leave home?'

'No.'

'Did you ever threaten him?'

'No.'

'Do you feel any remorse over his death?'

'Why should I? I didn't have anything to do with it.'

'You think you're a pretty cool customer, don't you? But to me you're just stupidly stubborn.'

Lester shrugged. He knew the police were hoping to needle him into making some damaging admission. At the outset of the interview he had experienced fright and near panic, but his mood had shifted into one of defiance and indifference. He felt himself armoured against whatever pressure they might apply. Taunts, threats and cajolery could no longer succeed. They'd never be able to prove he had anything to do with his stepfather's death.

For his part, Everson felt angry, frustrated and surprisingly unsure of himself. If Judge Holtby's death stood on its own, it could be seen as a straightforward case of suicide. Though no note had been found saying why he had decided to end his life, an explanation would normally be forthcoming. For the moment, however, there appeared to be no explanation.

But the trouble was that his death wasn't an isolated event. It had to be seen against the backcloth of the past week. The

154

dramatic demise of Mr Justice Ambrose had triggered off an unholy sequence of events and Judge Holtby's death fitted somehow into the pattern. Above all Everson was acutely conscious of the fact that he had charged somebody with Mr Justice Ambrose's death, and now this had happened to complicate things.

Even if Judge Holtby *had* committed suicide, what the hell was his stepson doing there and why couldn't the judge have left a note explaining his deed? It was Ian Lester's presence at the scene that most troubled him. He had told an unlikely story which would, however, be more plausible if he himself were a less ambiguous figure in the pattern of events.

Everson still had a trump card and decided that the moment had come to play it. He hunched himself forward and fixed Lester with a ferocious look.

'Care to say what you were doing on the courthouse balcony taking photographs that day? And why you've kept it a secret all this time?'

For several seconds Ian Lester merely gaped. Then slowly the colour drained from his face and with a small weird moan he slipped sideways off his chair and crashed to the floor.

Chapter 25

Rosa had been trying to get in touch with the police all day to tell them about her call from Mervyn. But she was always just missing them and being obliged to leave messages. For whatever reason, however, they never called her back and she was forced to conclude that she was low down on their list of priorities. She hadn't wished to mention Mervyn's name in the various messages she left, so it was true they didn't know what she wanted.

Around half past seven that evening she had just sat down in front of the television with a plate of scrambled eggs on her lap when the phone rang.

'It's Robin, Rosa. I've just heard that Tony Holtby's been found dead. Apparently shot himself in his car not far from home. One of our local officers came round to see me about defending his wife on a shop-lifting charge and mentioned it. He knew of our interest in recent events at Runnymede Court.'

'How awful!' Rosa exclaimed. 'I wonder what drove the poor man to do it, though he'd looked on the verge of a breakdown. There must have been a final straw.'

'The other interesting fact is that Ian Lester's at the station being interrogated by Everson. It appears he discovered his stepfather's body and then led the police a wild chase in his car.'

'Do you know which station he's at, Robin?'

'They're now at Colne, which itself is an interesting development. I mean, why take Lester there unless they

156

think he had some connection with other events?'

'Maybe the rumour that he's the missing photographer has filtered through and they're questioning him about that.'

'Possibly. Anyway that's the latest scene.'

'Thanks, Robin. I'll call Colne Police Station now and sit on the line until I get either Everson or Martin.'

'Preferably Martin.'

'Yes, though I'm prepared to take on Everson if need be.'

'I've never doubted your readiness to take on anybody,' Robin remarked. 'Call me back when you have some news.'

As things turned out, Inspector Martin came on the line with greater willingness than Rosa had expected.

'You messages have only just caught up with me, Miss Epton,' he said in a disarming tone, 'and I was going to call you at your office first thing in the morning. I'm afraid it's been a more than usually hectic day. Anyway, what can I do for you?'

Rosa decided that the tactful thing was to impart her own information before trying to elicit anything from him. Nevertheless she hoped to be able to draw him on the subject of Judge Holtby's death.

'I wanted to tell you about a phone call I've had from Mervyn,' she said.

'That's interesting. What did he have to say?'

Martin listened without interruption while she gave him the details of their conversation.

'So he suggested that Judge Holtby might have been the intended target on the balcony, did he?' he observed. 'Without knowing a bit more about Mervyn, in particular on whose side he is, one can't really assess the suggestion. It's clear he's not operating on his own. His call to you was almost certainly on somebody's instructions. The question is whose.' He paused and Rosa felt she could read his thoughts. He was deciding whether to mention Judge Holtby's death and, if so, exactly how much he should tell her. 'I don't know whether you've heard, Miss Epton, but Judge Holtby appears to have shot himself.'

157

'As a matter of fact, I had heard.'

'Ah! I thought the news might have reached you. It looks like suicide, but there are one or two puzzling features.'

'Did he leave a note?'

'Not that we've been able to discover. There really ought to be a law obliging genuine suicides to leave behind a written word of explanation. It would make our lives so much easier. I'm sure you agree.'

'I certainly do. It's often unfair on the living when they fail to do so.'

'Exactly.'

'I gather his stepson was involved in some way,' Rosa observed.

'News travels faster than light where you're concerned, Miss Epton.'

'Well, I'm naturally interested in view of my own client having been charged with murder.'

'Yes, naturally.'

'In what way was Ian Lester involved?'

'If it wasn't suicide, it was murder. And if it was murder, young Lester would be the number one suspect.'

'Speaking off the record, Mr Martin, do you think it was murder?'

'No. We're hoping that forensic and fingerprint tests will rule out that possibility.'

'But you'd still be left wondering why Judge Holtby took his life?'

'What would be your theory, Miss Epton? After all you saw much more of him recently than the police did. From all accounts he was a sick man.'

'If you ask me, he wasn't in a fit state to try our case, even though my client was the beneficiary.'

'Would he have got off anyway?'

'I can't imagine Mr Justice Ambrose would have let him slip through the net so easily.' After a pause she said, 'I have heard a rumour about Ian Lester that may or may not have reached police ears . . .'

'That he was the missing photographer?'

'So you have heard.'

'Sooner or later we hear everything, Miss Epton.'

'Have you questioned him about it?'

'Of course. His first reaction was to fall off his chair in a faint and his second to deny it.'

'Will you be holding an identity parade?'

Martin sighed. 'We'll be consulting the D.P.P. about that. And about various other matters as well.'

'Such as whether you've charged the wrong man with murder?'

'Your client was charged on available evidence,' he said firmly.

'May I ask if Ian Lester is still helping you with your enquiries?' Rosa asked in a sardonic voice.

'The answer to that, Miss Epton, is that he has left the station a free agent, but that our enquiries are continuing.'

'Into all aspects of the affair?'

'With you defending we have no choice.' Then quickly he added, 'Not that we want to do other than dig out the truth. The police aren't interested in cover-ups.'

Rosa felt like saying that everyone from governments down was interested in cover-ups when the truth was embarrassing and they thought they could get away with one, but decided it was better to remain silent.

'Is Bernard Blaker still your client?' Martin asked, breaking in on her thoughts.

'No-o. Why do you ask?'

'Should you come across any link between him and what's been happening to these judges, I'd be glad of a tip-off.'

'I see.'

'It seems to be more than a coincidence that everything began on the day his trial was due to start.'

The same thought had also occupied Rosa's mind.

'So any connection between him and what happened on the balcony might be the key we're looking for.'

'Mervyn could be a link in that chain.'

'I have it in mind.'

'I'll have to think about what you've just said,' Rosa said slowly. 'There is such a thing as professional confidence.'

'That's why I asked if he was still your client.'

For a while after he had rung off, Rosa stared in thought across the room. The conversation with Martin had given her thoughts fresh impetus. It was possible that the police possessed information denied to her, but it was also apparent they had no knowledge of the link between Blaker and Ian Lester.

Nor, of course, would she have but for one of those quirky interventions of fate.

Chapter 26

When, later that evening, she called Robin and told him what had happened, he struck an immediate note of caution.

'In my view a solicitor–client relationship still existed when you met Blaker at the Pastel Club.'

'Surely it terminated with his acquittal. It isn't even as if there's any question of an appeal to be considered.'

'Nevertheless I seem to recall your telling me that he wanted to see you on a professional matter but suggested a social setting as being pleasanter.'

'So?'

'So you can hardly tell the police what took place when you met him.'

'Surely there's a distinction between what we talked about and something that happened like Ian Lester's intervention?'

'I feel you're splitting hairs.'

'No, I'm not,' Rosa said indignantly. 'Supposing I'd recognised someone in the club whom I knew the police were looking for, an I.R.A. bomber for instance, are you saying I couldn't have breathed a word because I was with a client at the time?'

'I'm not saying anything of the sort. Of course you could have tipped them off. You wouldn't even have had to disclose who you were with at the time. It's a wholly different situation.'

'But the police would have wanted to know what I was doing in the club; who I was with and details of that sort. You know they would.'

'All right and assuming the I.R.A. bomber had no connection with Blaker, I'd see no objection to your giving them those details.'

'Supposing the bomber had waved to Blaker across the room, what then?'

Robin let out a laugh. 'I've told you what I think. We could go on arguing this and tossing it to and fro for the rest of the night.'

'After all,' Rosa went on determinedly, 'my number one interest is Nigel Ambrose. He's my client and I've got to look after him. Are you saying that, even if it became vital to his defence, I still couldn't reveal the link between Blaker and Ian Lester?'

Robin sighed. Though nobody less resembled a terrier in appearance, there was no doubt that Rosa possessed many of the qualities of one.

'I'm not saying that at all. It'd be a question of *how* you did it. There's always been more than one way of skinning a rabbit.'

'I know and I have an idea how I'm going to start skinning this one.'

'Don't say we've been indulging in all this moral flagellation for nothing!'

Rosa laughed. 'No, but I've formed an idea while we've been talking. I shall go and see Ian Lester myself.'

'And what'll be your approach?' Robin asked warily

'I'll drive down to the Holtbys tomorrow morning.'

'And if he's at home, what'll you say to him?'

'I'll play it by ear.'

'You'll still need to have an opening gambit.'

'I'll tell him who I am, what my interest is and I'll say that I recognise him from the Pastel Club.'

'You'll make a frontal assault in fact.'

'Yes.'

'You may have to contend with his mother.'

'I imagine she'll be mourning behind drawn blinds. She'll hardly want to receive any strangers.'

'You'll soon find out.'

'I'll also find out exactly what the connection is between Lester and Blaker,' Rosa said grimly. 'I'm more than ever sure that the wrong person has been charged with Mr Justice Ambrose's death.'

'It certainly sounds as if Ian Lester could have been implicated in some way.'

'And I'm going to discover what way.'

Rosa left home at eight o'clock the next morning. She reckoned it would take her about an hour to reach the Holtbys' house. Robin, who had once visited it, told her it was about two miles outside Chobham.

Nine o'clock might not be an acceptable hour for a social call, but then her visit scarcely qualified as such. She was anxious to catch Ian Lester before he went out, though from all accounts he was much more likely to be in bed than up and about at that time of day.

She found the address without too much difficulty and drove up to the front door. The house comprised three farm cottages knocked into a single dwelling with an additional modern extension at one end. It lay in a hollow about half a mile back from a secondary road.

It had a silent and deserted look as Rosa got out of her car and gazed for a moment at the long grey façade. The front door was situated at one end (the left hand cottage as one faced the house) and Rosa approached and rang the bell.

She was beginning to think that everyone must still be asleep, which would not be so surprising in the circumstances, when the door opened and a woman stood peering at her with infinite suspicion.

'Mrs Holtby?' Rosa said.

'I'm afraid Mrs Holtby's not well. Can I help you?'

'Actually it was Mr Lester I wanted to see.'

The woman stared at her with increased suspicion. 'Who are you?' she asked with scarcely veiled hostility.

'My name's Rosa Epton. I'm a solicitor from London.'

163

'I've heard my husband mention your name,' the woman said in a more friendly tone. 'I'm Heather Welford. My husband sits at Runnymede Crown Court. I came over yesterday evening to be with Mrs Holtby and I stopped the night.'

Rosa gave her a sympathetic look. 'I've recently been involved in a case before Judge Holtby and I've also met your husband.'

'I suppose you know that Judge Holtby's dead?'

'Yes, I heard last night. It came as a great shock. How is Mrs Holtby?'

'You're obviously not aware that Ian's also dead.'

'Ian Lester dead!' Rosa exclaimed in a stunned voice. 'I had no idea. When did it happen?' She shook her head in bewilderment. 'It seems to be one tragedy after another. Poor, poor Mrs Holtby.'

Heather Welford gazed at her in thoughtful silence. Then with sudden decision she said, 'Why don't you come in? I'm expecting the doctor to call a bit later, but meanwhile it'll be a relief to talk to somebody.'

She led the way into a long low room which ran the length of the whole house and which had a comfortable lived-in look about it.

Rosa perched herself on the edge of a chair. She had seldom felt so ill-at-ease and apprehensive. She had arrived in a mood of high determination and been immediately bowled over by the news of Ian Lester's death. What could have happened? Surely he had not followed his father's suicide with his own?

'Ian came home about eight o'clock yesterday evening,' Heather Welford said, sitting down opposite Rosa. 'He'd been at the police station several hours answering questions about his stepfather's death. It was he who discovered the body, you know.'

Rosa gave a small nod. It might not be exactly as Inspector Martin had told it, but what did that matter now?

'His mother was totally distraught by the news of her

164

husband's death and Ian went straight up to her bedroom and tried to comfort her. I stayed down here. When he appeared it was to say he was going out. He saw from my expression that I disapproved and he said rather quickly that he wouldn't be late. He said I needn't worry and that he'd told his mother, which, incidentally, I later found not to be true. Anyway he drove off in his car . . .'

'Did he say where he was going?'

'No. And I didn't feel it was my place to ask him. I assumed he was going out for a drink, which was understandable, but which, nevertheless, struck me as a thoroughly bad idea. Fortunately the doctor had left sedatives for Mrs Holtby and shortly after Ian had departed I persuaded her to take them and try to get some sleep. I sat up till after midnight before going to bed, but Ian hadn't returned.'

'You must have been anxious.'

'Not so much anxious as angry with him.' She paused and fixed Rosa with a puzzled look. 'Incidentally, Miss Epton, you've not told me why you wanted to see Ian. You must have had a compelling reason to come calling at breakfast time.'

'I represent Nigel Ambrose who, as you know, has been charged with murder,' Rosa said diffidently.

Heather Welford stared at her in wide-eyed surprise. 'I hadn't realised you were Nigel's solicitor. You obviously know that I was once married to Edmund Ambrose?'

'Yes.'

'I can't imagine what Nigel was up to that day,' she said in a distant voice. Then refocusing her gaze on Rosa she said, 'What's the connection between your representing Nigel and your wishing to talk to Ian?'

'I think Nigel's been wrongly charged and I hoped Ian could clarify one or two points.'

'You don't think it was Ian who shot at my ex-husband?'

'I don't know,' Rosa said with a sigh. 'I'm in the business of exploring motives and opportunities.' Heather Welford

165

appeared to become lost in thought and after a pause, Rosa went on, 'You were saying that Ian had not returned home by the time you went to bed around midnight . . .'

'No, he hadn't. And then around five o'clock this morning the phone rang and I answered it. It was the police saying that a car, thought to be Ian's, had been involved in an accident and had caught fire and the driver had been killed. About half an hour later a sergeant and a constable arrived at the door and I let them in. Denise was still asleep and I decided not to wake her. Coming on top of the earlier shock I dreaded to think what effect the news of Ian's death might have on her. They said the car had failed to take an S-bend about two miles from here, had plunged into a bank and caught fire. The driver had obviously been unable to get out and was burnt to death. They assumed the accident had been caused by drink. I gather the car was a total write-off, but they were able to identify it by one of its number plates which had fallen off.'

'What a ghastly thing to have happened!' Rosa said with a shudder.

Heather Welford gave her a harrowed look. 'And I've not yet told Denise Ian's dead. At the moment she thinks he's in hospital following an accident. And that's bad enough. I phoned the doctor as soon as the police had gone. Luckily he's a personal friend of the family and came immediately. He gave her a further sedative and she's still asleep.' She stared unseeingly across the room before adding, 'I'm not sure it wouldn't be best if she never woke up.' After a slight pause she went on, 'That's a terrible thing to have said! After all she still has three children to live for.'

'Can they be got hold of?'

'Charles, who's the oldest, is cycling with a friend somewhere in France and Susan's camping with her boyfriend in Wales. And Paul's at school, but he's only fourteen. I'm hoping Susan may get in touch later today when she hears the news of her father's death. On the other hand it's quite likely she's not looking at newspapers or

166

listening to the radio. All I can do is cross my fingers and hope that either she or Charles will hear by one means or another.'

'Are you expecting the police to come back?'

'They're bound to.'

'Who reported the accident?'

'Some people who live about a quarter of a mile from the scene saw the glow from their bedroom window and phoned the Fire Brigade. That was shortly after half past three.'

'I wonder where he'd spent the evening,' Rosa remarked thoughtfully. 'He can't have been drinking in a pub all that time, so what was he doing?'

'I know he'd recently been causing his parents a great deal of worry. He'd disappear for days on end and they wouldn't know where he was. My own guess is that he kept some fairly disreputable company.'

Rosa nodded slowly. Including that of my recent client, she reflected.

A silence fell which was broken by Heather Welford saying, 'What do you think really happened, Miss Epton? Life's been a nightmare ever since Runnymede Crown Court opened. My poor husband never deserved all this.'

'I realise what a strain it must have been for everyone,' Rosa said sympathetically.

'It seems to have the inexorability of a Greek drama, but where's it going to end, Miss Epton? Where's it going to end?'

Though Rosa didn't aspire to answer that heartfelt question, she thought she now had a better idea of why it had all started on that breezy, sunny day out on the balcony of Runnymede Crown Court with the swollen river rushing past beneath. Not every piece fitted neatly, but an overall picture was emerging.

She glanced enquiringly at Heather Welford as she heard a car pull up outside.

'That'll be the doctor.'

'Then I'll depart,' Rosa said. 'It's been a great pleasure

167

meeting you, even in these unhappy circumstances. I don't wish to add to Mrs Holtby's troubles, so don't tell her of my visit unless you feel you must.'

Heather Welford nodded vaguely, her mind clearly preoccupied with the grim prospect ahead.

As she got into her car Rosa decided to make a detour and visit the scene of the accident, Heather Welford having given her directions.

She was stopped by a uniformed constable at a junction short of the S-bend and informed that the road ahead was temporarily closed. The officer looked nonplussed when she told him who she was, though he hesitantly agreed that she might leave her car on the verge and proceed on foot.

On rounding the bend a hundred yards ahead she saw a parked police car and a group of people standing around, including the familiar figure of Detective Inspector Martin. As she approached he glanced round and rewarded her with a look of total surprise.

'You certainly get around, Miss Epton,' he said in a tone of grudging respect as she came up to where he was watching two officers taking measurements and two others collecting items of debris and carefully dropping them into polythene bags.

'I've just come from the Holtbys' house,' Rosa said. 'Mrs Welford has told me what happened.'

'And what are you doing here at this hour of the morning anyway?' he enquired.

'I wanted to have a talk with Ian Lester.'

'I should have guessed.'

She followed his gaze in the direction of the wheel marks that scored the soft verge. It was about three feet wide with a two foot deep ditch on its far side. Beyond the ditch was a solid grass bank. All around the foliage had been blackened and there was still a smell of burnt oil and rubber to assail the nose. The car had already been taken away for examination, as had the body of its hapless driver.

It was possible to see from the marks just how the accident

had occurred, the car mounting the verge and ramming the bank on the farther side of the ditch. The impact had presumbly been such as to set it off like a fire bomb.

'I hope it was a quick death,' she murmured with a shiver.

'I doubt whether he knew very much about it. If anything.'

There was something in Martin's tone that caused Rosa to give him a puzzled glance.

'Because he was so drunk, you mean?' she said.

'Possibly. But possibly not.' He gave Rosa a speculative look. 'I'm not sure why I'm telling you this, Miss Epton, except that we've been fairly frank in our exchange of information to date and I suppose I hope that co-operation will bring me a further dividend.' He gave a small, quizzical smile before going on, 'A quick, preliminary examination suggests that this wasn't a case of spontaneous combustion. In other words, the car was deliberately set on fire.'

'And Ian Lester burnt alive?' Rosa exclaimed in a horrified voice.

'My guess would be that he was already dead. The post mortem should be able to establish whether or not that was so, though his body was so badly damaged by the fire that it'll probably require detailed tests of the surviving organs before we know the truth.'

'You think he may have been killed before being driven here and the car set alight?'

'Yes.'

'I suppose it was Ian Lester's body?'

'Yes. We got his dentist out of bed at what he considered an ungodly hour this morning and he produced Lester's dental chart. Fortunately, he's a local man and Mrs Welford found an appointment card with his name in Lester's bedroom. There seems no doubt it was Lester in the car all right.'

Rosa gave an abstracted nod as Martin watched her intently. Raising her eyes and meeting his gaze, she said, 'Here's your dividend, rather sooner, I imagine, than you'd expected. There's a link between Ian Lester and Bernard Blaker. I can prove that they knew one another.'

Chapter 27

Bernard Blaker sat grim-faced in the drawing-room of his house near Weybridge. The new hi-fi equipment for which he had recently paid £5000 sat silent in its corner and the thirty-inch screen of his television set was as blank as a prison wall.

He gazed at the pictures hanging on the walls, a Bonnard, a Dufy and a Matisse, not to mention the Renoir which was the only one he really liked, but found no pleasure in what he saw. They were mere investments, outward and visible signs of his wealth.

He was all alone in the house which was a rare enough event at any time. His wife, now permanently estranged, was, he believed, somewhere in the South of France. Gail, his mistress, was up in town, but would be back later. Monty Yarfe was in Amsterdam looking after a drugs deal and Douglas, his chauffeur-cum-bodyguard, was down at the local pub.

He got up and went across to the Sheraton sideboard that discreetly housed an array of bottles and glasses and fetched himself a fresh drink.

It had always been one of his rules never to employ what he called amateurs. Another had been to keep the smaller fry in his organisation well away from him. He considered these two rules essential to safeguarding his position. But now he had broken both and was living to regret it. For not only had Ian Lester been an amateur in the worst possible sense, but he had allowed him to get far too close in personal terms. As

170

events had proved, he was a thoroughly unstable youth and therefore a menace.

He reflected bitterly that if the police and Customs people hadn't got him on that flimsy drugs charge, everything would be much better than it was. Events had got out of hand almost as soon as he had been charged. They had, of course, been trying to nail him for ages, but they never had the evidence. They didn't really have any on this recent occasion, but had nevertheless plunged on like intoxicated bloodhounds.

His acquittal had cost him dearly, not merely in money, and the full consequences of his trial were still incalculable.

It was Gail who had first met Ian Lester at a party a week or two after the four of them had been charged with their drugs offence. She had formed the view that he might be worth cultivating in view of his father's position and his own eagerness to obtain hard stuff.

She had arranged for him to meet Blaker who had shared her view of his potential. Thereafter his seduction ensued as Blaker began to supply him with small amounts of cocaine for which he waived all payment, so that Ian Lester could scarcely credit his good fortune.

When, however, Blaker proposed a return for his investment, Lester showed himself in his true colours, which were those of a frightened little boy. It had had to be made clear to him who held the whip hand and what would happen if he failed to fulfil his side of the bargain. The fact that he had been unaware of any bargain was irrelevant. Spiders don't waste time arguing with flies once they've flown into the web.

Blaker cursed himself for not having foreseen how quickly Lester could switch from being an asset to a liability. At the time he had entered their lives, however, he had every appearance of being an answer to a prayer.

He put down his glass and pushed it away. Even his favourite Napoleon brandy had a sour taste this evening. He knew that the police were bound to interview him about

171

Lester's death. They would have learnt of the link between the two of them and would pummel and probe it in their own fashion. Not that they'd be able to prove anything. Douglas had assured him that both car and driver were no more than charred remains. But Blaker knew what miracles of detection modern science could achieve in such cases and was a good deal less sanguine than his bodyguard.

He felt no remorse about Ian Lester's death. It had become a necessity and Douglas had strangled him with all the artistry he had learnt as a commando. It had been a swift, almost painless death.

From the moment Lester had arrived at the house unheralded the previous evening, it was clear that he had become a danger to them all. He had been in a highly charged emotional state. His father's suicide, followed by his lengthy questioning by the police, appeared to have completely unhinged him.

Killing him had been like putting down a pet for which no cure was possible.

The telephone began to ring, splintering the silence that enveloped the house. He let it continue for a while before rising from his chair and going to answer it.

'That you, boss?' a familiar voice enquired. 'It's Mervyn. I was wondering if you wanted me to call that lawyer girl again?'

'No,' Blaker said curtly and hung up.

172

Chapter 28

'If you ask me, everything's rotten in the state of Denmark,' Everson observed. 'And in case you don't recognise it, that's a quotation.'

'I'm sure even Shakespeare would recognise it – more or less,' Martin replied with a grin.

'I've never known a case with more red herrings,' Everson went on grumpily.

'In my view we can now ignore most of them, sir. I mean, people like Mr Leo Dodd and Mr Keffingham may have held grudges against Mr Justice Ambrose, but there's absolutely no evidence they did anything to kill him. The same goes for Judge Welford. He may have written a silly, threatening letter to old Ambrose, but that was years ago and, if anything, it gave the judge a reason for murdering Mr Welford, rather than the other way round.'

'The fact that Ambrose kept the letter all these years proves something.'

'It proves he wasn't someone to let bygones by bygones. He bore his own grudges and carefully stored away any ammunition that fell into his hands. Of course we'd never have known about that letter had his housekeeper not found it and decided we ought to see it. I suppose we'll have to do something with it in due course.'

'Lose it,' Everson remarked promptly.

Martin smiled at the incisiveness in his chief superintendent's tone.

'Are you now satisfied, sir, that Judge Welford's brother is

173

in the clear?'

'Satisfied?' Everson grunted as though the word had a disagreeable flavour. 'I still think he's behaved suspiciously. And he had as much opportunity as anyone else out on that balcony.'

'But what motive?'

'What motive did anyone have?'

'I believe, sir, that if one looks at everything that's happened, and I mean everything, it all forms part of a mosaic.' Martin drew a deep breath as he awaited Everson's reaction.

'Well, get on with it and don't be so ruddy poetic.'

'Thanks to Miss Epton's tip-off we know now there was a link between Blaker and Judge Holtby's stepson. It's my bet that what took place out on that balcony was in some way connected with Blaker's trial. I suspect that something went wrong along the line and thing's didn't work out as intended, but I believe that's the starting point.'

'Before you go on,' Everson said in a grating tone, 'tell me how Nigel Ambrose fits in to your theory?'

'I'd like to leave Ambrose on one side for the moment, sir,' Martin said with a note of cajolery.

'I'm sure you would, but he happens to be charged with murder. He's not on one side. He's plumb in the centre of your so-called mosaic.' With a sudden impatient gesture he went on, 'It's time we stopped talking and acted. We're going to visit Blaker and find out just what his relationship with young Lester was.'

'If he tells us anything at all, we can be pretty sure it won't be the truth.'

'Provable lies are often better than the truth,' Everson remarked with a tight, tigerish smile.

Chapter 29

'I don't deny that I knew Ian Lester,' Blaker said quietly, giving the officers a somewhat sad and resigned look. He had not expected them to arrive on his doorstep quite so swiftly, but was determined to appear unconcerned by the visitation. 'I didn't know him well, but I knew him,' he went on. 'I've nothing to hide. I bet you thought I'd send for my lawyer before agreeing to talk to you.' He made an expansive gesture with his hands. 'But here I am alone in my home, offering you my co-operation.'

'How long did you know him?' Everson asked stonily.

'Only a few months. Miss Bristow met him at a party and introduced him to me.'

'You knew, of course, that his stepfather was a judge at Runnymede Crown Court?'

'Certainly I did. He told me that.'

'Did you mention your connection with Judge Holtby to anyone before your trial began?'

Blaker frowned. 'Connection? I don't follow you. I had no connection with Judge Holtby. I'd never seen him in my life until I stepped into his court. And I'm sure he had no idea who I was, apart from being a defendant in a case he was trying.'

'Did it ever occur to you to try and put pressure on him?'

'Pressure? What sort of pressure are you talking about?'

'To try and influence the conduct of the trial.'

'Are you seriously suggesting that I tried to bribe him?' he asked incredulously. 'Because, if so, that's the most fanciful

175

idea I've ever heard. Anyway, aren't British judges supposed to be incorruptible?'

'I'm not suggesting that money changed hands . . .'

'Thank you, at least, for that!'

'But you could still have tried to influence the course of your trial.'

'Naturally I tried to influence it, but through my lawyers and within the rules of the game. How else?'

'By getting Ian Lester to put pressure on his stepfather on your behalf.'

Blaker's tone was scornful when he replied. 'I wasn't aware he had any influence over his stepfather. He told me they didn't get on very well. Anyway why should Ian have done what you suggest when I scarcely knew him?'

'Because you demanded a return for the favours you'd done him,' Everson said grimly.

'What favours?'

'Hadn't you supplied him with drugs?'

'Really, chief superintendent! I'm not a street corner pedlar of drugs.'

'But you agree you had a much easier run in front of Judge Holtby than you would have had before Mr Justice Ambrose?'

Blaker let out an exaggerated sigh. 'I'm told so, but as I'd never come across either gentleman before I can only give you what I believe is called a hearsay answer.'

'Do you agree that Judge Holtby appeared to be a sick man during your trial?'

'Yes, but are you blaming me for that?'

'Did Ian Lester come and visit you here last night?'

'No.'

'Did you see him at all last night?'

'No.'

'When did you learn of his death?'

'My chauffeur heard of it in the local when he was having a lunchtime drink.'

'What was your reaction?'

'One of surprise and shock. It's terrible to think of a young man dying in that way.'

It was clear to Inspector Martin that they were not going to get anywhere. They hadn't sufficient ammunition and Blaker knew it. Martin had been against the visit on that very ground, but Everson had hoped a shock tactic might produce results. It might have done with someone less tough and resolute than Blaker. As it was all Everson's questions had bounced back like rubber balls off a wall.

'I can see you're interested in gadgetry,' Martin remarked amiably in the silence that followed.

Blaker gave him a suspicious look. 'What are you referring to?' he asked warily.

'Your hi-fi and video equipment. And I couldn't help noticing your sophisticated burglar-alarm system when we arrived.'

'This is one of the most burglarised areas in the south of England and I own a lot of valuable pictures and other things.'

'But you still have a fondness for electronic toys?'

Blaker made a self-deprecating gesture. 'You could say so.'

'Do you do a lot of photography too?'

'No.'

'I'd heard you had a small private cinema here,' Martin went on in the same friendly tone.

'I have, but that doesn't mean I shoot the films myself. Photography as such doesn't interest me,' he said with an air of finality.

Shortly afterwards, as the officers got up to leave, Martin suddenly turned back and said, 'By the way do you know somebody called Mervyn?'

'Mervyn?' Blaker shook his head. 'I don't think I know anyone of that name.'

'A coloured man.'

He shook his head again. 'I'm afraid the answer's still no.'

177

Chapter 30

'It has to have been him,' Rosa said when she met Robin in the office the next day. 'Only Ian Lester fits all the facts. Obviously Blaker had some blackmailing hold over him, presumably drugs, and supplied him with the fake camera . . .'

'Why wasn't he recognised? There must have been several people present who knew him.'

'Because he had on some sort of disguise. But his stepfather recognised him, I'm sure of that.' She fixed her partner with a compelling look. 'The whole thing makes sense, Robin, once you accept that it wasn't necessarily the intention to kill Mr Justice Ambrose. All the plan required was to put him out of action so that he wouldn't try the Blaker case and it would go back into Tony Holtby's list. The poison pellet would have achieved that object even if it hadn't resulted in his death.'

'So you're suggesting that Tony Holtby was fixed?'

Rosa nodded. 'I'm sure he was put under pressure to ensure that Blaker and his co-defendants were acquitted. I suspect he was told that not only would his stepson be otherwise exposed, but that it would be done in such a way as to make his own resignation from the bench imperative. Only that can explain why he appeared to be under such a heavy strain during the trial and why he did make sure the case was chucked out. It also explains why he subsequently committed suicide. The poor man was no longer able to live with his conscience knowing what he'd done.'

'You make it all sound very logical, Rosa, but you're overlooking one vital feature . . .'

'No, I'm not,' Rosa burst in. 'Nigel Ambrose's part, you mean?'

'Yes. How do you account for him?'

'He was just a diversionary tactic. I think he drifted into the picture quite fortuitously and was exploited.'

'Go on, explain!'

'Accept that Mervyn was obviously one of Blaker's men. He happens to meet Nigel in the Queen's Head shortly before the trial was due to start at Runnymede Crown Court. Nigel mentions he's a nephew of the judge going there and Mervyn reports this to Blaker, who sees a splendid opportunity of creating a bit of extra confusion. Ian Lester would already have been given his role, but if Nigel could be persuaded to go along with a camera ostensibly to play a trick on his uncle this would provide a diversion to the main operation. As events turned out, Nigel was putty in their hands. He was only too willing to do anything for ready cash and not to ask too many tiresome questions.'

'As I recall, it was pure chance he was recognised by one of the catering staff. Supposing he hadn't been?'

'You can be quite certain the word would have been put around one way or another that he was there. Nigel was the perfect fall guy.'

Robin looked thoughtful for a while. 'You've certainly got it all worked out, the only question is whether it's correctly worked out.'

'Fault it!'

'I can't at the moment. Incidentally, I assume Mervyn's phone call to you suggesting that Tony Holtby was the intended victim, and not old Ambrose, was merely another diversionary tactic.'

Rosa nodded keenly. 'What the intelligence services call disinformation. A false story to conceal the truth and sow confusion.'

'So what now?'

179

'I must get hold of Martin and tell him.'

'Supposing he doesn't accept your reconstruction of events?'

'He will. He must, because it has to be the truth.'

Chapter 31

Thirty-six hours after her husband's death and twenty-four after that of her son, Denise Holtby got up to face a new day.

Considering the double shock she had suffered, followed by all the heavy sedation, she felt surprisingly alert and ready to cope with the aftermath of what had happened. She knew there would be police enquiries and inquests: indeed, the police had already been to visit her. They had been tactful and brief, but had made it clear they would wish to see her again.

Heather Welford had departed the previous evening after being assured that Susan could look after her mother's needs.

It was one of those sunny mornings with a stiff breeze, not unlike that which had prevailed on the opening day of Runnymede Crown Court. A day that now seemed to belong to another lifetime.

The two most important men in her life were dead, awaiting Christian burial once the coroner released their mortal remains. But even this macabre reflection failed to distract her busy mind.

What had most disturbed her was Tony's failure to leave any sort of farewell note. She had searched all their favoured hiding-places without avail. Now she was waiting to speak to his solicitor about the arrangements that would have to be made. She was determined that husband and son should be buried together in a joint ceremony.

She paused in the act of putting on some perfume (Givenchy that Tony had given her at Christmas) and burst

181

into sudden tears. Then quickly repairing the damage to her face she went downstairs to make herself a cup of strong black coffee.

For thirty-six hours she had lain on her bed, drifting in and out of sleep, and totally uninterested in the outside world. Now she must face life again and couldn't afford the luxury of continuing self-pity. She had never been a person to let matters follow their own course as long as she had any power to direct them.

She knew that her husband had taken his own life. Moreover, she knew why. As for Ian, he had fallen into the hands of wicked men who had been responsible for his death and who would sooner or later be brought to justice. The police had promised her this would be so.

She glanced at her watch. It was only just after six o'clock. Too early to expect a solicitor to be in his office.

Gordon Churston was the senior partner of Reeves, Findy and Pexo, solicitors of Lincoln's Inn Fields.

He had been Tony Holtby's solicitor for over twenty years and the two men had been friends since their days at university. In recent times their professional dealings had been mostly by letter or over the phone and social contact consisted of visits to one another's homes two or three times a year.

At the time of Judge Holtby's death, Churston had been staying with a wealthy and mildly eccentric client in the more remote part of Cumbria. One of his eccentricities was a refusal to take a national newspaper, so that news of the judge's death passed him by. It was not until his wife phoned him on the evening before his return to London that he was told what had happened.

He had immediately called the Holtbys' house and spoken to Heather Welford, saying that he would get in touch with Denise as soon as he was back in his office, a day that coincided with her revived interest in survival.

He reached his office on the dot of nine thirty the next

182

morning and went up to his spacious room on the first floor that overlooked the square. Miss Foster, his secretary of many years, had, as usual, arranged his mail in what she considered to be proper order, something she arrived at by a mixture of intuition and prescience, coupled with a careful study of handwriting, postmarks and quality of stationery.

On top of the pile on this particular morning was a hand-addressed envelope which he instantly recognised as coming from Tony Holtby. It was marked *Personal and Strictly Private* in the top left-hand corner. He picked it up with a slight feeling of apprehension and weighed it in the palm of his hand. It certainly contained more than a single sheet of paper.

Slitting the envelope with a silver paper-knife he extracted the contents. There was a letter which began *Dear Gordon* and two sealed envelopes. One was addressed to *H.M. Coroner* and the other to *Gordon Churston Esq* which was marked, *For Your Eyes Only*.

The first letter read:

Dear Gordon,

By the time this reaches you, I'll be dead by my own hand.

Please pass the enclosed letter to the coroner which will simplify his task. It merely tells him I am proposing to take my own life in a fit of deep depression and contains all he needs to know in order to return the required verdict.

The envelope addressed to you is, as it says, for your eyes only. It's an explanation of my death which I feel obliged to leave behind, but which I ask you not to divulge to anyone. I hope this is not placing an unfair burden on you, but I've always regarded you as one of the most discreet and resourceful men I know and I'm sure you'll cope with your customary skill. It'll probably be best if you eventually destroy it, but I had to say it all to somebody and you're my chosen repository.

Please give Denise all the help you can. She'll need it. As you know I love her as much now as the day we first met.

With my heartfelt thanks to you, Gordon,

Yours,
Tony

Churston laid down the letter and picked up the sealed envelope that was addressed to him. For half a minute he merely stared at it while there flashed through his mind a kaleidoscope of all the occasions he and Tony Holtby had shared over the past thirty-five years. He had not seen him for a couple of months or more, but was, of course, aware of the events that had taken place at Runnymede Crown Court. He had dropped him a short note of sympathy, expressing the hope that it might yet prove to be the happy posting he had so much looked forward to. He had received no reply (nor expected one) until now.

With a sudden, swift gesture he slit the envelope and pulled out the two folded sheets of paper.

Dear Gordon, he read.

> *The decision to end my life is not a sudden one. Indeed, it might have been better if I'd done it sooner. The truth is that I have dishonoured my profession and degraded my judicial oath and I can no longer live with my conscience. Let me just say that I came under pressure to ensure the acquittal of certain defendants in a drugs case. The alternative, I was told, was to face family disgrace or possibly worse. I succumbed, but it was not until I stood on the court balcony on that opening day that I realised how far the tentacles of corruption had reached. Since then it has been one continuing nightmare. If I had foreseen the full extent of all the ensuing horror I would never have embarked on such a slippery path. How often have I heard that from defendants in my court!*

Even now in the shadow of death I cannot bring myself to spell out every detail. Let admission of my own odious and unforgivable part be sufficient!

Support Denise in the days ahead and, for her sake, do what you can for Ian.

Yours,
Tony

Churston laid the letter down on top of the other and stared unseeingly across his room. When his phone buzzed it was a while before he lifted the receiver.

'Yes?' he said in an abstracted tone.

'I have Mrs Holtby on the line,' his secretary said.

'Tell her that I've just left the office and am on my way to see her. Say I expect to be there between eleven and eleven thirty.'

'I think she'd like to have a word with you now,' Miss Foster said a trifle reprovingly.

'No. Just give her that message.'

It was apparent to Gordon Churston that Tony Holtby had not known of his stepson's death at the time he wrote the letters and this for the very good reason that he was then still alive. All that Churston knew as he drove down to Chobham that morning was that Ian Lester's body had been found in his burnt-out car following an accident. It was only when he arrived that he learnt otherwise.

He had always been fond of Denise and had been appalled by what had happened. He dreaded meeting her in the light of the double tragedy that had shattered her life. Moreover her husband's letter contained a number of *lacunae* which didn't make his task any easier. Come to that, he wasn't sure exactly what his task would be, apart from offering sympathy and practical help over immediate arrangements.

He had taken a quick look at Tony's will before leaving the office and confirmed that the bulk of the estate was left to Denise and thereafter to his own three children. There was a legacy of £500 to Ian, but Churston had always understood

185

that he was provided for by his paternal grandparents, who had paid for his education and upbringing.

He had barely parked his car before the front door opened and Denise came running out. She flung her arms round his neck and embraced him warmly.

'Dear, darling Gordon,' she murmured in a choked voice, as she clutched his hand and led him indoors.

'I hardly know what to say,' he murmured back. 'Winifred and I are both distraught at what's happened.'

It was soon clear that all she wanted was to pour out her heart and all he had to do was sit back and listen. When she told him the police suspected that Ian had been murdered, he could only shake his head in stunned disbelief. Used as he was to seeing people at times of personal crisis and tragedy, this seemed totally beyond acceptable reality.

'I am so upset, Gordon, that my Tony never left a note. Not a single word of farewell. We'll never know why he did it.'

'As a matter of fact he did leave a note,' Churston said awkwardly. 'He wrote me a letter which I found waiting for me in the office. In fact he wrote me two letters, as well as one to the coroner.'

Denise's hands flew up to her face as she stared at him with an expression of alarm.

'He wrote you a letter?' she whispered dramatically.

He nodded. 'He said he felt he had to explain everything to someone before taking his life.'

'And he told you everything?' she said in a histrionic tone, at the same time jumping to her feet and walking over to the window. She stood in silence with her back to him for a while, as slim and upright as when she'd been a girl. Then with a tremor in her voice she said, 'I wasn't telling you the truth when I said just now that I didn't know why he killed himself. I did know. Although he never hinted by so much as a word, I *knew* that he'd recognised me on the balcony. I saw it in his expression as I pointed that silly camera at Edmund Ambrose.' Gordon Churston felt his blood run suddenly cold as he realised what she was saying. It was as if he was listening at a keyhole where he had no right to be. Denise clearly assumed that her husband had told him this in his letter. She now went on, 'Poor Ian lost his nerve and couldn't go through with it, so I did my dressing up bit as a young man and took his car.' With a note of pride she added, 'Once an actress, always an actress! You see we had to make sure Tony would try that case, though the poor love had no idea what was afoot that day. Once Ambrose said he wanted the case, I think Tony was almost relieved. But it couldn't be left like that, or they'd have made sure Ian went to prison and Tony would have been disgraced anyway.' She swung round and faced her solicitor. 'I mayn't look tough, Gordon, but I am where my family's concerned.' She paused and her shoulders suddenly sagged. 'So what are you going to do with the letter?'

'Destroy it,' he said without hesitation. 'That's what Tony asked me to do.'

He got up and walked over to the log fire where he dropped the pages of the letter one by one into the dancing flames, watching them swiftly crinkle and turn to ash.

He found that his knees were trembling as he straightened up and returned to his chair.

Should the police come asking him questions, they would learn nothing. He had carried out his client's wishes.

'I'm glad Tony told you everything,' she said quietly. Then after a pause: 'Do you think I ought to give myself up?'

'Who will that help if you do?' he remarked after a moment's silence. 'Let's wait and see what the police do in the next few days. Provided we don't connive at a positive miscarriage of justice, I think that sleeping dogs could be allowed to lie.'

Chapter 32

Three days later on the afternoon before Nigel Ambrose was due to appear on remand in the Magistrates Court, Rosa received a telephone call.

'Miss Epton?' a clipped, rather military voice enquired. 'This is John Waddington of the D.P.P.'s department. Thought I'd let you know we shan't be proceeding further against your chap when he comes up in court tomorrow.'

'You mean, he'll be discharged?'

'Precisely.'

'I'm very pleased to hear it. What's happened to produce this decision?'

'We've had an opportunity of conferring with the officers, and taking everything into account the Director has decided to drop the case.'

'Does that mean somebody else may be charged with the same offence?'

'Can't answer that, Miss Epton. Anyway, least said soonest mended in this sort of situation, eh? See you at court tomorrow.'

When Rosa told Robin of this sudden turn of events he raised his eyebrows in surprise and said, 'Things have certainly moved very swiftly.'

'Do you know John Waddington of the D.P.P.'s office?'

'The major?' He laughed. 'I don't know whether he ever actually was in the army, but he looks and talks the part. You'd better give your buttons an overnight polish or he'll have you on a charge.'

188

When she arrived at court the next morning, she found the building under virtual siege. The press had got wind of what was going to happen and had turned up hungry for drama.

She fought her way inside and made for the jailer's office where she asked if she might see her client.

Nigel Ambrose gave her one of his slightly shifty smiles as they greeted one another.

'I hear I'm to be released,' he said without particular animation.

'Yes, I'm delighted to say. I'm sure it'll be a great weight off your mind.'

'As a matter of fact, I've quite enjoyed my week in Brixton prison. Now I'll have to look around for somewhere to go.' He gave her a hopeful flicker of a look. 'Any chance of compensation?'

'I'm afraid not.'

'Pity, because all I've got in the world is five pounds. But I'll manage somehow. After all, I'm a survivor, aren't I?'

It was later as she made her way into court that an officer waylaid her.

'A lady asked me to give you this, Miss Epton,' he said, thrusting an envelope into her hand. She opened it to discover five £10 notes inside. There was also a note which read:

Dear Miss Epton,
*   Please give this to Nigel, but don't tell him where it came from!*
*   Best wishes,*

Yours sincerely

Heather Welford

John Waddington lived up to his telephone image and within five minutes everything was over. Uttering a string of brisk clichés which he somehow managed to make sound the epitome of practical common sense, he asked the court to

189

discharge the defendant.

As he sat down, he turned to Rosa and whispered, 'Had a word with the clerk beforehand. Always best to fix these things behind the scenes. Avoids unseemly argy bargy in open court, eh!'

Rosa almost expected the observation to be accompanied by a smart clap on her back.

She was one of the last people to leave court and found Inspector Martin waiting for her by the door.

'Didn't have a chance to speak to you beforehand,' he said. 'The last few days have been one hectic rush.'

'You've even left me breathless,' Rosa remarked with a smile.

'We suddenly began to have a few breaks. The main one was tracing Mervyn. That was particularly fruitful as we found him in a fairly disenchanted mood with his boss.'

'Blaker?'

'Yes, as we'd both suspected. Mervyn's told us that the camera he passed to your client was a perfectly ordinary one and that Ambrose was used purely as a diversionary tactic.'

Rosa let out a satisfied sigh. It was always nice to have one's theories proved right.

'What I might call the lethal camera was supplied by Blaker for use by Ian Lester. We've still got a long way to go with our enquiries, but there doesn't seem to be much doubt that the whole exercise was a gigantic and elaborate attempt to pervert the course of justice.'

'One that succeeded, too,' Rosa remarked.

'I promise you Blaker won't get off a murder charge so easily. Even if he still has you to defend him, Miss Epton.'

Rosa recoiled in mock horror. 'That's one case you won't find me in,' she said firmly.

'Well, I have to be going,' Martin said. 'But meanwhile thank you for your help.'

'Thank you for yours.'

Martin gave her an amused wink before turning on his heel.

While they had been talking, Rosa had noticed a tall, grey-haired, smartly-dressed man hovering nearby. He now approached her.

'My name's Gordon Churston, Miss Epton. I'm the Holtbys' family solicitor. If it's not too glib a comment to make, everything seems to have reached as satisfactory a conclusion as was possible after such a succession of tragic happenings.'

'I suppose you could say that.'

'I've had a word with Chief Superintendent Everson and the police seem convinced that Ian Lester was the culprit.'

'That's a strange word to use in respect of somebody who goes about firing poison pellets at judges.'

'One pellet at one judge,' Churston said in a gently reproving tone. 'At all events I'm greatly relieved for everyone's sake that Ian is now out of it, tragic as his own death may be.'

Rosa nodded. 'It certainly solves a lot of problems,' she remarked.

'Quite so, Miss Epton. Quite so.'